I0692423

PATTY'S PLEASURE TRIP

Patty's Pleasure Trip

BY
CAROLYN WELLS

AUTHOR OF
TWO LITTLE WOMEN SERIES,
THE MARJORIE SERIES, ETC.

GROSSET & DUNLAP
PUBLISHERS   NEW YORK

CONTENTS

CHAPTER I

FUN AT THE GRANGE

"YES, indeed," said Patty, pleasantly.

"And then a broad-leafed hat, with ribbons from the edge of the brim, tied under my chin,—or, perhaps chiffon ties. Which would you have, Patty?"

"Yes, indeed," said Patty, in a voice of enthusiasm, but not looking up from her book.

"Oh, Patty, you silly! Now, listen. Look at these plates, and pick out the prettiest hat so I may get it for the garden-party."

Lady Kitty spread out the sheets of millinery designs, and still absorbed in her reading, Patty lifted her hand and, without looking, pointed a finger at random till it rested on one of the pictured hats.

"That one! Why, Patty, you're crazy! I couldn't wear that pudgy little turban,—I want

[9]

a big sun-hat. Would you have a straw or lace?"

"Yes, indeed," said Patty, turning a leaf and devouring the next page of her book.

"Angel child! You think you're teasing me, don't you? But not so! I love to see you so bent on literary pursuits! Indeed, I don't think one book at a time is enough for a great brain like yours,—you should have two at once. You go on with yours, and I'll read another to you."

Picking up a book from a rustic couch near by, Lady Kitty began to read aloud. Her reading was more dramatic than the text warranted, and besides much elocutionary effect, she gesticulated vigorously, and finally rose, and standing straight in front of Patty, kept on reading and declaiming in ludicrous style.

The two were under a large marquee, on the lawn of Markleham Grange, the country home of Lady Hamilton, and her father, Sir Otho. Patty was comfortably tucked up among the cushions of a lengthy wicker chair, and had elected to spend the morning reading a new story-book of the very kind she liked best. So, partly because she didn't want to be disturbed, but more for the sake of mischievously teasing her friend, Patty pretended to be oblivious to the hat subject.

But she could not long keep a straight face while Kitty waved her arms and trilled her voice in ridiculous fashion, as she continued to read aloud from the book. Then she would drop into a monotonous drawl, then gallop ahead without emphasis or inflection, and sometimes she would chant the words in dramatic recitative.

Of course, while this went on, Patty couldn't read her own book, so finding herself beaten at her own game of teasing, she closed the volume, and said quietly:

"I wish you'd let me advise you about that new hat you're thinking of buying. You always selects such frights." As Lady Hamilton's hats were renowned for their beauty and variety, this speech was taken at its worth, and in a moment the two friends were earnestly discussing the respective merits of chiffon, lace, and straw, as protection against the rays of a garden-party sun.

It was the latter part of a lovely morning in the latter part of a lovely August. Patty had drifted through the summer, making and unmaking plans continuously in her efforts to

[11]

secure the greatest good to the greatest number of her family and friends. She had not joined her parents in Switzerland, as she had thought to do, for invitations to various English country-houses had seemed more attractive, and after a round of such parties, Patty had come to Markleham Grange, for the double purpose of having a few quiet weeks, and of being with her adored friend, Lady Kitty.

The Grange was a typical country home, with all the appurtenances of terraces, gardens, duck-ponds, woodlands, and hunting preserves.

In the great, rambling house guests came and went, and Patty greatly enjoyed the personal freedom that prevailed.

Though occupations and amusements of all sorts were provided, no social obligations were exacted until afternoon tea time. At five, how-ever, everybody assembled on the lawn, or, if rainy, in Sir Otho's billiard-room, and the host himself accepted the attention and companion-ship of his guests. Dinner, too, was rather formal, and there was always pleasant enter-tainment in the evening. But it seemed to Patty that she liked the mornings best. She strolled, often all by herself, through the woods and parks; she chatted with the old gardener about the rare and beautiful flowers; she played with the pet fawns, or idly drifted about the lake in a small rowboat. Sometimes she met Sir Otho on her morning rambles, and for a time they would chat together. The old gentleman had a decided liking for Patty, and though he was an opinionated man, and dictatorial of speech, the girl's innate tactfulness kept her from rousing his contradictory spirit, and they were most amiable friends. But, perhaps best of all, Patty liked the mornings when boxes of new books arrived from London.

Selecting an interesting story, she would make a bee-line for her favourite reading-place. This was a large tent-like affair, canopied, but without sides, and furnished with wicker chairs, tables, and lounges. Soft rugs covered the ground, and the view was across a small lake, dotted with tiny, flowery islands, to glorious green woodlands beyond.

Here, Patty would read and dream until the all too short morning had flown away, and a servant, or Lady Kitty herself, would come to summon her to luncheon. And it was here that Lady Kitty came, with her sheets of new hat designs, just up from London, when teasing Patty declined to be interested.

[13]

But having at last thrown herself into the discussion it proved to be an animated one, and ended by Lady Kitty's return to the house to send an order for hats for both of them.

Patty remained in her lounging chair, but did not immediately resume her book. Her thoughts flew back to Kitty's ridiculous antics as she read aloud to tease Patty. Then her gaze wandered out to the lake, and she watched a flock of ducklings, who were enthusiastically paddling along by the side of their more sedate mother. Such funny, blundering, little balls of down they were, and when one of them nearly turned a somersault in its efforts to swim gracefully, Patty laughed aloud at him.

" Do it again! " said a low but commanding voice at her side, and Patty looked round to see a grave-looking young man seated on the arm of a chair.

She had not heard him approach, and she stared at him with a pardonable curiosity. He was garbed in white flannels, with a soft, white, silk shirt and Windsor tie.

Though most correct in manner and bearing, he yet had an informal effect, and his large dark eyes looked almost mournfully at Patty.

Fun at the Grange

"I said, do it again!" he repeated, in a slightly aggrieved tone.

"Do what again?" said Patty, more astonished than offended.

"Make that funny noise,—something like a laugh; *was* it a laugh?"

"Why, yes; one of my very best ones. Didn't you like it?"

"I thought it was a chime of fairy bells," was the reply, so fervently given that Patty laughed again.

The young man solemnly bowed as if in acknowledgment of her kindness.

"Don't take it so hard," she said, smiling; "you'll get over it; you'll be all right in a moment."

"I'm all right now, thank you. I get used to things very quickly. And,—by the way,—you don't mind my talking to you? Without having been properly introduced, I mean."

"I do mind very much. I think you're forward and unconventional, and I hate both those traits."

"You're so direct! Now, a softer, subtler insinuation would have pleased me better."

"But I'm not trying to please you!"

"No? You really ought to study to please."

[15]

The young man arose and looked at Patty with an air of calm, impersonal criticism. "It would suit your personal appearance so well."

"Indeed! What *is* my personal appearance?"

"Ah, direct and curious, both! Well, your beauty is of the sort described in most novels as 'not a classic face, or even good-featured, but with that indescribable charm'——"

"Indeed! I've been told that my features were very good."

"Ridiculous nonsense! Why, your eyes are too large for your face; your hair is too heavy for your head; and, and, your hands are too little for anything!"

"How rude you are!" said Patty, shaking with laughter, "but as I brought it on myself, I suppose I oughtn't to complain. Now, let's drop personalities and talk commonplaces."

"Awfully mean of you—before I had my innings. However, I don't care; let's. It's a fine, well-aired morning, isn't it?"

"Are you always so funny?" asked Patty, staring at the young man, like a child pleased with a new toy.

"'Most always," was the cheerful retort; "aren't you?"

Fun at the Grange

"Now you're rude again, and I must ask you to go away. But tell me your name before you go, so that I may avoid you in future."

"What a good plan! My name, on the Grampian Hills, is Floyd Austin, and, truly, I'm well worth knowing. This performance this morning is just an escapade. Into each life *some* escapades must fall, you know. And, by the way, if you'll disentangle your eyes from my gaze just for a minute, and look the other way, you'll see the august Sir Otho coming, with ' bless you, my children ' written legibly in every line of his shining morning face."

Sir Otho came toward them with hearty greetings.

"Well, well, Patty," he said; "so you already know our friend Austin? That's good, that's good! But you must be afraid of him, for he's one of our coming poets. He's already a celebrity, you know."

"Are you a celebrity?" demanded Patty, turning to Floyd Austin.

"I am," he said, gravely, "why?"

"Why are you one?"

"To pay a bet," Austin replied, so promptly that his two hearers laughed.

[17]

"He's crazy," said Patty to Sir Otho; "I never heard such talk!"

"He's a humorist, my dear child; you don't know his language."

"A humorist?" said Patty, turning to Austin with simple inquiry on her pretty face. "I thought you were a poet."

Austin flashed an amused look at Sir Otho, and then looking at Patty, he said, in a smooth, even voice:

"'The force of Nature could no further go,— To make myself she joined the other two.'"

"I do understand your language," cried Patty, gaily, "that's in Bartlett,—and it says, 'Under Mr. Milton's Picture'!"

"Oh, my dear Patty," said Sir Otho, "is your poetical knowledge bounded by Bartlett?"

"But, Sir Otho," observed Floyd Austin, in his slow, quiet way, "Bartlett is not such a bad boundary. His book is like a bird's-eye view of a city,—which is always a good thing, for one can then pick out the churches and monuments so easily."

"Yes, and one can miss the most interesting bits that lurk in narrow streets and obscure corners."

Fun at the Grange

"True enough, and so we both have the best of the argument."

Floyd Austin was a popular favourite, and one of the explanations of his popularity lay in the fact that he rarely continued to disagree with any one. The discomfiture of another, which is so pleasing to some clever people, was positively painful to his sensitive nature, and so easily adaptable were his own opinions, that he could adjust them to suit those of another with no trouble at all. This made his character somewhat indefinite, but added to the charm of his personality, and his sunny good nature was a quick passport to the good will of a new acquaintance.

One of Austin's minor interests was harmony of colour. He looked at Patty as she stood leaning lightly against the back of the chair from which she had risen at Sir Otho's approach. She wore a long summer cloak of a light tan-coloured silk, lined with another silk that was pink, like a seashell.

Simply cut, the long full folds almost hid her white frock, and she gathered the yielding material about her with a graceful gesture.

"How well you wear that cape, Miss Fair-

[19]

field," said Floyd, and then turning to Sir Otho, he asked, " Doesn't she? "

"Why, yes; I daresay," said the older man, uncertainly. " Do you, Patty? "

" I don't know," said the girl, laughing. " I hope so, I'm sure, for it's one of my favourite wraps. Are you an artist, Mr. Austin, that you're so observant? "

" I'm an artist in most ways, yes," he replied; " and I love colour better than anything else in the world. Those two shades in your cloak, now, are like——"

" Like coffee and strawberry ice cream," put in saucy Patty, and young Austin agreed enthusiastically.

" Just that," he cried, " and surely there's no better combination."

" I like lemon, myself," began Sir Otho, and just then Lady Hamilton came trailing her soft frills across the lawn toward the group.

" Floyd Austin! by all that's wonderful! " she exclaimed, as she held out both hands to the young man, and smiled a welcome.

" Yes, Lady Kitty," he said, taking her hands, and smiling an acceptance of her welcome, " and so glad to see you again."

[20]

Fun at the Grange

"Is Mr. Austin a long-lost brother?" asked Patty, "and if so, why have I never heard of him before?"

"Yes, he's a brother of all the world," said Kitty; "the very dearest boy ever. I believe he lives next door to us, but he's never there, for when he's there he's always here!"

"Oh, is he Irish?" said Patty, and Floyd Austin's eyes twinkled at her quick repartee.

"He's cosmopolitan," said Sir Otho; "lives all over the world. But he's a dear vagabond. and as long as we can keep him here, we're going to do so."

"Not long," said Austin, shaking his head. "I'm just down for a whiffling trip, and then off again to a summer clime."

"Oh, you can change your plans," said Lady Kitty, easily. "I've known you to do it before. And I'm sure I can persuade you now, for I've Miss Fairfield to help me coax you."

"Oh, I'm no good at coaxing," said saucy Patty, who was not yet quite sure that she liked this rather audacious young man.

"But I'll teach you how to coax prettily," he said; "and then when you learn, you can coax me to do anything, and I'll allow myself to be persuaded."

"Allow yourself indeed!" said Patty. "Probably you won't be able to help yourself!"

"Probably not," he responded, with his unfailing concurrence.

CHAPTER II

A SUMMONS HOME

AFTERNOON tea was in progress, and as a light rain had set in, it was being served in the billiard-room.

This large apartment was very attractive, for aside from the purpose for which it was intended, it was admirably adapted for a cosy lounging-place. A sort of extension with roof and sides of stained glass was an ideal place for the tea-table and its many appurtenances, and except for the footman, who brought in fresh supplies, Lady Kitty and her guests waited upon themselves.

Though never a large group, a few neighbours usually dropped in at tea-time, and as there were always some people staying in the house, the hour was a social one.

Patty, looking very dainty in a pretty little house-dress of Dresden silk, was having a very good time.

[23]

Flo Carrington, a young English girl, whom she had met only the day before, came bustling in with exclamations of dismay.

"I'm nearly drowned!" she cried. "The pelting rain has ruined me frock, and I'm starving for me tea. Do give me some, dear Lady Kitty."

"You shall have it at once," declared Patty, hovering around the tea things; "cream or lemon?"

"Lemon, and two lumps. You pretty Patty-thing, I'm so glad to see you again. I've only known you twenty-four hours, but already I feel one-sided if you're not by me. Sit down, and let's indulge in pleasant conversation."

So with their teacups, the girls sat down, and being largely about their two selves, the conversation was very pleasant indeed. But soon they were interrupted, as Cadwalader Oram, a typical young Englishman, approached them.

"You two young women have monopolised each other long enough," he declared; "you must now endeavour to entertain me."

"That's easy," said Patty, and turning to a near-by muffin-stand, she took a plate of hot,

[24]

buttered ones, and offered them to young Oram;
"have a muffin?"

"Indeed I will, they're very entertaining.
Have you ever noticed how wonderful the
Markleham muffins are? I get such nowhere
else. Why is that, I wonder?"

Lady Kitty, who was waiting by, answered
this herself.

"Because at large and formal teas," she said,
"muffins are not served; and if one's friends
drop in unexpectedly, muffins are rarely ready.
It is my aim in life to have just so many people
to tea as will justify muffins without prohibiting
them."

"At last I understand why the teas at this
house are always perfection," said Oram, rising
for a moment as Lady Kitty moved away.

A newcomer had arrived, and Patty, looking
up, saw Floyd Austin's grave face in the
doorway.

"Owing to the inclemency of the weather,
the starving people gathered in the billiard-
room to partake of that nourishment which was
to keep them alive until the dinner hour."

He said this in an impersonal, reading-aloud
sort of voice, which seemed to Patty extremely
funny.

"He's always doing that," said Flo Carrington; "sometimes he's screamingly droll."

After greeting his hostess, Austin made his way toward the small group clustered round Patty.

With much chat and banter, he was served with tea and muffins, and so much attention was shown him that Patty concluded he must be a favourite indeed.

"I fear we have rudely run into a cloud-burst or something," remarked Cadwalader Oram, unsuccessfully trying to look through a window, whose stained glass was further obscured by slipping raindrops.

"Sit down, Caddy," said Flo; "you mar the harmony of this meeting when you're so restless."

"Being thus admonished, young Oram crumpled himself gracefully into a chair," drawled Floyd Austin, as Oram did that very thing, and Patty's laughter rang out at the apt description.

"Do that again," said Austin, looking gravely at Patty, but she only smiled saucily at him, and looked over his head at another man who was approaching.

"Mayn't I be invited to join this all-star

group?" If the speaker's voice betokened a confidence in his own welcome, it was not misplaced, for smiles of greeting were bestowed on him, and Flo Carrington moved to make room for him between herself and Patty on the great settle.

"Striving to act as if a literary lion were an everyday occurrence, the ladies beamed graciously upon him," droned Austin; and so pat was his allusion that they all laughed.

"This is Peter Homer, Miss Fairfield," said Flo, and Austin added:

"Beyond all doubt, the most outrageously interesting man you have ever met."

"Just queer enough to be delightful," put in Cadwalader Oram, and Mr. Homer smiled benignly at the chaff flung at him.

"He isn't queer at all," declared Flo; "he's a genius, and a thoroughly sensible man."

"Both? Impossible!" exclaimed Floyd Austin.

"Not at all!" said Mr. Homer, himself. "I'm writing a book in twenty volumes, Miss Fairfield,—that proves my genius. And I've left my work to come and chum with my friends, —that proves my sense."

"What is your book about?" asked Patty,

[27]

a little uncertain how to talk to this wise man. "Tell me about your work."

"How can I talk to you of work," said Mr. Homer, "when you don't even know what the word means? Have you ever done any work in your life?"

"No," admitted Patty; "I'm too busy being idle to have any time for work. My life is nothing but folly."

"But folly and happiness are twins," said he looking kindly at the girl, and when kindness shone in Peter Homer's blue eyes he was indeed attractive.

"They are," agreed Patty; "but pray how do you know what the word folly means?"

"His folly is being wise," broke in Cadwalader Oram.

"Good for you, Caddy!" exclaimed Floyd Austin. "If that didn't have a vaguely familiar ring about it, I should say you'd made an epigram."

"Well, let's say it all the same," said Flo Carrington; "he may never come any nearer to one."

"I don't want to," returned Oram. "Stevenson says, 'There's nothing so disenchanting as attainment,' and that's a delightful principle

[28]

A Summons Home

to work on. I hope to goodness I shall always fail just as I'm about to attain."

"What nonsense!" cried Patty. "Then if you ever ask a lovely girl to marry you, you'll be secretly hoping she'll say 'no!'"

"My word! but Americans are clever!" said Mr. Oram, bowing to her; "but for the sake of my argument, I must even subscribe to that."

"Oh, pshaw, Caddy!" said Mr. Homer, "don't worry over it. You know you're a younger son, and very few girls would marry you anyway."

"Very few would be enough," observed Cadwalader, quickly and Floyd Austin immediately chimed in:

"Having neatly vanquished his opponent, the younger son chuckled softly to himself."

Then as Lady Kitty came, and took Mr. Homer away, the little group broke up and somehow Patty found herself talking to Floyd Austin.

"Say some more of those funny things," she demanded; "I never heard any one do that before."

"The young man glanced furtively at his watch, and a spasm of pain crossed his features

[29]

as he realised he must say adieu to the fair young girl before him."

Austin said this in a whimsical, high-pitched tone, and Patty laughed aloud in spite of herself.

"Thank you," he said, earnestly, for his admiration of her musical laugh was now a standing joke between them. "And by the way, there's a dance at Three Towers to-morrow night. I suppose you'll go. Will you give me all the odd-numbered dances? Just for luck, you know."

"All the odd numbers! Why, I never heard of such greediness! I'll give you just one dance, and you may be thankful if you get all of it!"

"Somehow, I can't feel alarmed, for I know you'll change your mind a dozen times before to-morrow night comes."

"How well you read me! But truly, I can't help it. I always fraction up my dances, and they won't come out even, and then I have to tear up my programme, and then of course I can't remember who's who in the ballroom."

"Who's hoodooed in the ballroom, you mean. But after that programme's torn up, I may fare better than in the face of its accusing statistics."

"Tell me something about Mr. Homer," said

[30]

Patty, as she looked at the tall man who was the centre of an admiring group.

"Peter Homer? Well, he's the rightest kind of a fellow, a great scholar, and the best-looking man I ever saw,—outside my own mirror."

"Do you think you're pretty?" asked Patty, looking at him with an air of innocent inquiry.

"Yes, indeed. Not as pretty as you are, of course, but still a beauty. But Homer has the noble brow and lantern jaws that go to make up the ideal of facial elegance. Isn't his hair stunning?"

Mr. Homer's hair was black and abundant. It was somewhat bushy and of coarse texture, and was tossed over back, as if by the incessant pushings of an impatient hand.

"You'll like him," Austin went on, "but you won't understand or appreciate him; you're too young and ignorant."

"Thank you," said Patty.

"Not at all. Don't mention it, no trouble, I assure you. But Homer's a puzzle."

"I'm specially good at puzzles."

"Ah, but he isn't of the 'transposed, I am a fish,' variety. You never can solve Peter Homer, little girl."

[31]

"I've no desire to," said Patty, a little chagrined at his superior tone. "He isn't a prize puzzle, is he?"

"With the native quickness of the young American, she gracefully took the wind out of the sails of the conversation," piped Austin, as he looked at her admiringly. Just then a footman brought a telegram to Patty.

"I brought it at once, ma'am," he said, "if so there might be an answer. The man will wait a bit."

"Allow me," said Austin, slitting the envelope for her; "and I'll stand in front of you while you read it, lest it may be of dire import, and your emotion be exposed to the gaping crowd."

Patty smiled at his nonsense, and read the telegram:

"Last call. No more postponements. We will come for you next week, and all start for home September first. Be ready.

"Father."

"Oh," cried Patty in surprised dismay, as she grasped the sense of the message.

A Summons Home

"Can I help?" said Austin, quite serious now, for he saw Patty was really agitated.

"No. It's nothing tragic. At least, not really so, but it seems so to me. I have to go home, that's all."

"Home? to America?"

"Yes; and of course, I'm glad to go, in some ways, but I wanted to stay over here a little longer. Through the autumn, anyway."

"It's a beastly pity. I don't want you to go. Who says you must?"

"My father," said Patty. "I've been promising to join him all summer, but somehow I didn't get off, and now he suddenly says we're all to go home."

"All?"

"Yes, father and Nan and me. Nan's my dear little stepmother. She's the sweetest thing,—I just love her. I'm really crazy to see them both again, but I don't want to go back to New York quite yet. I'll soon get used to the idea, but coming just now, it's a disappointment."

"It is to me, I assure you. Why, we're just beginning to be friends."

"Yes, I shall always remember you pleasantly."

[33]

Patty was really thinking of something else, and said this so perfunctorily that Floyd Austin drawled out:

"Having made a polite speech, the young lady promptly forgot the very presence of the gentleman who was addressing her."

"Nonsense," said Patty laughing; "there, I'll put this rather disturbing telegram away for the present, and devote my attention entirely to you!"

"Heaven be praised!" murmured Austin, rolling his melancholy eyes toward the ceiling. "But oughtn't you to answer it? You know the henchman awaiteth."

"Oh, yes; well, I'll scribble a reply."

Turning to a desk, Patty quickly wrote:

"All right. Come on. I'll be ready."

Then addressing it, and signing it, she gave it to Floyd, who went in search of a footman.

After the tea guests had all gone, Patty went to Lady Kitty's room to tell her the news.

"Wake up," said Patty, gently dropping a kiss on the closed eyes of her friend, who was resting a bit before dinner.

A Summons Home

"What for?" asked Kitty, not opening her eyes.

"What for, indeed! To see the last of your rapidly-disappearing friend and partner. Eyes, gaze your last! Heart, breathe your fond farewells!"

The big blue eyes of Kitty Hamilton slowly unclosed themselves.

"Melodramatics, my dear!" she said; "what do they mean?"

"Read that!" said Patty, handing her the telegram.

Kitty read it twice, and then sat up, wide awake enough now.

"My little Pattypat," she said, "you can't go away home to America. I won't let you!"

"You can't help yourself, Kitsie. If father has made up his mind,—and it does sound so,— off we go."

"They're coming here next week," went on Kitty, musing over the telegram. "That part of it's delightful. I'll make it so pleasant for them that they can't tear themselves away."

"You can't do that, dear. But it will be fun to see them. Blessed old Nan! I've missed her a lot this summer."

[35]

"You fraud! I do believe you're glad you're going home, after all."

"Well, in some ways, I am. You know I'm rather adaptable, and when I get my sailing orders, I begin to face toward the sea. I hate to leave you, and lots of other friends over here, but, I have friends in America, too, you know. And, Kitty, Sir Otho promised he'd bring you over there some time."

"Well, perhaps he will. At any rate, don't let this summons cloud your bright young life for the moment. Lock it up in your desk, and put it out of your mind for to-night, anyway. Now, run and dress for dinner. What are you wearing?"

"Are there guests?"

"Yes, a few. Nobody very especial. Put on that speckled gauze thing."

"Don't you call my dotted chiffon by disrespectful names," and Patty ran, singing, away to her own room.

CHAPTER III

A PLEASURE TRIP OFFERED

"KITTY, I've had a jounce," said Patty, next day, as she sought her friend and found her in the pleasant morning room that overlooked the rose-garden.

Lady Hamilton treated her young guest to a haughty, disdainful stare.

"If you will talk in barbaric jargon," she said, "you can't expected civilised people to understand you."

Patty had an open letter in her hand, and as she fell sideways into a big easy-chair, she gave her hostess a dear little smile of apology.

"It is horrid, I know," she said, contritely. "I don't know why the excessively correct and well-bred atmosphere of Markleham Grange should bring out my worst American slang, but it does. I beg your pardon, Kitty, and I'll try to mend my ways."

"Oh, don't take it too seriously," laughed Lady Kitty, "and now, what *jounced* you?"

[37]

Patty's Pleasure Trip

"Well, you may remember I had a telegram yesterday, from my adored parent, telling me I was to start for home the first of September."

"I remember it with startling distinctness."

"Well, forget it, then, for it isn't true. One of the clever operators of your clever British telegraph company must have misread or miswritten a word, for I have a letter here from my father, and it seems he wrote *Rome* instead of *home*."

"Oh, Patty Fairfield! And aren't you really going home at all? And are you going to Rome? To Italy?"

"Yes, just that! Father and Nan have suddenly decided to spend the autumn in Italy, a pleasure trip, you know, and go straight to Rome first, and then go home later, about Christmas, they think."

"Well, I don't wonder you were,—what did you call it? Bumped?"

"No, I didn't say that. I merely announced that I was,—ahem,—surprised a bit."

"And pleased?"

"Yes, very much pleased. I didn't care a lot about Switzerland, but I'm crazy to go to Rome and Venice and some few other Italian

[38]

show-places. Indeed it will be a pleasure trip for me."

"Well, it's lovely. I can't leave now, of course, but father and I will run down to see you later, wherever you are. I need a little southern sun on my complexion."

"Nothing could improve your complexion," said Patty, kissing it, "but it will be great to have you join us. I feel like a whirlpool. It's awful to have my outlook whipped about so often and so suddenly."

"And to-morrow you may get a letter saying this is a mistake, and your father is taking you to Kamschatka."

"Indeed, it isn't father who's changeable! It's that bright telegraph operator, who can't read a gentleman's handwriting. Well, there's no harm done, and now I'll run away and adjust my mind to my changed fortunes."

Patty went out to her favourite seat under the awning, and gave herself up to day dreams of the delightful trip in store for her.

She had always longed to go to Italy, but had not expected to do so for many years yet. For some reason Mr. and Mrs. Fairfield had changed their plans, but though the letter told of this, it told little else.

"No hanging back now," her father had written; "no excuses of week-ends or house-parties. Cancel all your engagements, if you've made any, and be ready to leave Markleham Grange when we come for you next week."

"He needn't have been so explicit," thought Patty, "for I've no desire to put house-parties ahead of a trip to Italy. Why, I wouldn't miss it for anything! I wonder if we will go to Venice. I suppose I ought to study up art and things,—I'm fearfully ignorant. But I couldn't learn much in a week. I guess I'll wait, and learn it on its native heath. Perhaps I won't care much for the old statues and things, anyway. I suppose they're awfully ruined. Must look like a railroad accident. Oh, that's horrid of me! I ought to have more respect for such things. Well, I'm going anyhow, and I'll have the time of my life, I know I shall."

Patty lived through that day absent-mindedly. Somehow, going to Italy seemed a responsibility, and one not to be undertaken thoughtlessly.

She hinted this to Lady Hamilton, and Kitty laughed outright.

"My word!" she said; "don't you think

you're going to do the Yankee Tourist effect! Don't you go pottering about the galleries with your nose in a catalogue, and a Baedeker under your arm! A nice pleasure trip that would be! You're too ignorant to be an intelligent art lover, and not ignorant enough to pose as one; just stumble around among the pictures, and much of what is good will stick to your memory, and the rest will brush off of itself."

"You're a comfort, Kitty," said Patty; "I thought I ought to study up Ruskin on the Tuscans and Etruscans, or whatever those art books are about."

"You're too much of a goose, Patty, to study anything. But I expect you'll get a lot of fun out of Italy."

"I rayther think I shall," said Patty, with twinkling eyes; for, as she well knew, she found fun wherever she looked for it.

That night they went to the dance at Three Towers. This was a neighbouring country place, whose three noble towers ranked among the oldest in England. Patty was enchanted with the grand old house, for her delvings into architectural books through the summer had taught her to appreciate historic mansions.

Patty almost held her breath as she entered

[41]

the stately ballroom, with its crystal chandeliers, like suspended frozen fountains, sparkling with hundreds of wax candles. The floral decorations were elaborate, but to Patty's mind they almost detracted from the grandeur of the massive beams and studded ceilings of the fine old hall. After greeting the hostess, the Markleham party found themselves surrounded by friends and acquaintances, and Patty learned that the dancing had already begun.

Sir Otho made his escape to some other room, where he might chat undisturbed with some of his cronies, and Lady Kitty and Patty were soon provided with programmes, and besieged for dances.

"Now you *have* done it!" was Floyd Austin's comment, as he presented himself, and gazed in frank admiration at Patty's pretty evening gown of fluffy white tulle, decorated with silver tracery. "Is that the frock of a hundred frills?"

"Aptly named, Floyd," said Lady Kitty; "and a becoming costume for my little girl, isn't it?"

"Oh, fair,—madame, fair," said Austin, teasingly.

"I'd rather be asked to dance than to have

[42]

ambiguous compliments," said Patty, tapping her foot in time to the Viennese music of the orchestra.

"Come, then," said Austin, in a tone of patient resignation. "Shall I humour her, Lady Kitty?"

Smiling assent was given, and the two joined the dancers on the polished floor.

"How different from dancing in America," said Patty, as they wound slowly in and out among the circling throng.

"It's different from anything, anywhere, any time," said he.

"You're too vague," she sighed. "I never know whether you're making fun of me or not. Don't I dance right?"

"Right You dance like—like——"

"Now I know you're trying to think of a pretty allusion. Do get a good one."

"Yes, I will. You dance like,—why, very much like I do! We're both ripping good dancers."

Patty laughed out at this. "It *is* a compliment," she said, "though not just the sort I expected."

"Girls expect so much now-a-days. There, the music's stopped! Must I take you back to

[43]

Lady Kitty, or will you give me the next
dance?"

"Take me back, please. But later on, if
you care for another dance, you may come back,
—if you like."

"I *do* like. I think you were made for men
to come back to. Ah, Lady Hamilton, here is
your fair charge. Not a frill missing of the
original hundred, which speaks well for my
guardianship, as many of the ladies are ruefully
regarding tattered *chiffons,* so crowded is the
dancing floor."

"Will you trust yourself to me, then?" said
another voice, and Patty turned to see Peter
Homer smiling at her.

"Yes, Mr. Homer," she said, "as soon as I
get my programme again. Mr. Austin has it.
Oh, here it is. Yes, you may have this one."

And rosy with the fun of it all, Patty put
her hand on Mr. Homer's arm and walked
away.

But he led her away from the dancers to an
adjoining room, where there were fewer people,
less light, and no music.

"Sit down here and talk to me," he said,
arranging a chair for her. "I don't care for
dancing at all."

A Pleasure Trip Offered

"Well, upon my word!" said Patty. "But I do care for dancing."

"Yes, I know you do. But just now you're going to stay right here with me; so you may as well accept it gracefully."

"Why should I want to do that?" said Patty, who always rebelled at coercion. "Everybody else is smiling and gay, while you look like 'cloudy, with showers'!"

"Oh, no, I don't," said Mr. Homer, smiling; "and now what shall I talk to you about?"

"Italy," said Patty, promptly. "I'm going there soon. I don't know a thing about it, and I want to know it all. What's it like?"

"Well, Italy is like a lovely Monday in the spring; when they've washed the sky, and blued it, and hung it up in the sunshine to dry."

"That's pretty," said Patty, approvingly. "And are there trees?"

"Yes; trees tied together with long ropes of grapevines. They look like Alpine travellers roped together for safety."

"What are they really tied for?"

"They're not tied. The grapevines are festooned from one tree to another in the orchards. Thus it is a vineyard and an orchard both."

"It sounds lovely. Tell me more."

[45]

"No; I would rather hear you talk. Tell me what you want most to find in Italy."

"Beauty."

"There's plenty of that. Italy is a saturated solution of beauty. Which kind do you want, art or Nature?"

"I know so little about art. A lady at luncheon to-day was surprised because I don't even know the names of the twelve 'world-pictures.'"

"World-pictures! What are they? The scenes of Creation?"

"Why, a list of twelve of the greatest pictures in the world."

"My word! there's no fool like an art fool. But you're too chameleonic to go to Italy, anyway. It has some several hundred sides, and you'll absorb a bit of every one of them, and come back a mosaic, yourself. I wish you could concentrate, but I suppose you're too young."

"I'm not so dreadfully young, and—I am not bred so dull but I can learn."

"Well, learn right, then. Don't let them teach you to rave over Botticelli's 'Spring,'— go and look at 'David' instead."

"Mightn't that be merely a difference of individual taste?"

A Pleasure Trip Offered

Mr. Homer frowned. "Yes, it might be," he said; "have you an individual taste?"

About to be offended, Patty thought better of it, and smiled.

"What a dear disposition you have," said Homer, in a tone full of contrition. "I have a brutal way of speaking, I know, and I am so sorry. But I wish I could show you Italy as you should see it."

"Everybody seems to want to show me Italy as I should see it," observed Patty, placidly.

"Yes, and you'll get a fine jumble of it! Italy is half glory and half glamour, and you'll be so rolled up in the mists of glamour that you can't see the glory clearly."

"I hope I shall," exclaimed Patty. "I want the glamour. I want to see the Coliseum by moonlight. I don't care how hackneyed it is!"

"You oughtn't to see it by moonlight. You ought to see it at midday, in the strong, clear sunlight; and all alone, listen to its vibrant silence that tells you of itself."

"Oh," said Patty, thrilled by the intense note in his voice. "I didn't know you had so much imagination."

"That isn't imagination, it's reality. The real past speaks to you; not a foolish emotional

[47]

reproduction that you have conjured up your self."

"The curfew tolls the knell of our next dance," chanted Floyd Austin, coming toward them. "I thought I never should find you, Miss Fairfield. May I have you, please?"

"Mr. Homer is telling me about the Coliseum," said Patty, making no move to go.

"Quite right, quite right. If any one has anything to say, he may as well say it about the Coliseum. But that is liable to stand for some time yet, and this witching hour is fleeting. So, cub, oh, cub with be,—the bood is beabig."

Patty rose, laughing.

"I suppose I must go," she said, as Mr. Homer bowed courteously, and murmured a few words of regret at her departure.

"Another victim?" said Austin, quizzically. "Now, how can a will o' the wisp like you attract a wise and solemn old owl like Homer?"

"He attracted me," said Patty, simply.

"Oh, that explains it. But then, you also attract people who do not attract you; myself, for instance."

"Why, I think you're quite pleasant," said saucy Patty, looking at him with an air of patronising indifference.

A Pleasure Trip Offered

"You'd better think so, or I won't be pleasant!"

"Oh, yes, you will; you're always pleasant."

"As Rollo's uncle said to him, 'It's a pleasure to go about with such a pleasant and sensible boy as you.'"

"But I didn't say sensible."

"Thank Heaven for that! Now never mind remembering what Homer told you about the Coliseum, but remember what I tell you. Be sure to see it by moonlight first. The night I first saw it, the moon was gibbous——"

"What does gibbous mean?"

"I haven't the slightest idea. But, anyway, the moon was awful gibbous, and the moonlight was misty, like spray, you know,—and it flooded the Coliseum, and ran over onto the dome of St. Peter's——"

"What nonsense are you talking? You can't see St. Peter's from the Coliseum, can you? Have you ever been to Rome?"

"Now that you mention it, I don't believe I have! But what's the use of imagination, if you can't see things you've never seen?"

"You are too ridiculous!" declared Patty, laughing, and then nodding him a dismissal, as Cadwalader Oram claimed her for a dance.

[49]

"How she is made for happiness," said Austin, as he dropped into a chair beside Lady Kitty, and together they watched Patty dance away.

"She is," agreed Kitty, who was a life-long friend of Floyd Austin, and greatly liked the young man; "yet she's not nearly so much of a butterfly as she seems."

"I'm sure of that,—though I've only seen her butterflyish side. If Meredith hadn't already used the phrase, 'a dainty rogue in porcelain,' I should coin it to describe Miss Fairfield. Don't tell me she has an aim in life."

"Not quite that; but I think sometimes she wishes she had one."

"You mean, she thinks she ought to wish she had one."

"Yes, that is a truer statement of the case," agreed Kitty.

CHAPTER IV

A FAREWELL PARTY

MR. and Mrs. Fairfield arrived duly at Markleham Grange, and in response to urgent invitation consented to stay there for a few days before taking Patty away with them.

But the last evening had come and the party that gathered on the terrace after dinner showed that subdued air that last evenings usually compel.

The party was not a small one, for there had been guests at dinner, and several of the young people from the neighbouring country-houses had come over later, to say good-by to Patty.

"I'm so sorry to have you go," said Flo Carrington, as she possessed herself of Patty's hand and caressed it.

"I'm sorry to go," replied Patty; "somehow it seems as if I were always saying good-by to somebody. I've visited so much this summer, and every visit means a regretful parting."

[51]

"At the heartrending pathos of Miss Fairfield's tones, everybody burst into tears," declaimed Floyd Austin, burying his face in a voluminous handkerchief. But so burlesque was his woe that everybody burst into laughter instead.

"You may stay here if you choose, instead of going with us, Patty," said her father. "I didn't realise it would be such a wrench for you and your friends."

"No, thank you," said Patty, decidedly. "The longer I stay, the more painful would be the wrench,—and I've no notion of losing my Italian trip, anyway."

"That's the right way to look at it," said Austin, approvingly, "and cheer up, the fatal blow is yet to fall. I, too, am going to Italy in a few weeks, and I'll meet you on any Rialto you say."

"Are you really?" exclaimed Patty, pleased at the prospect. "Won't that be gay, father? And Lady Hamilton and her father are going later too. We can have a reunion. Won't you come, Flo?"

"I wish I could," said the girl, and Mr. Fairfield said heartily:

"I shall be more than glad to welcome any

of Patty's friends, wherever we meet them. When are you starting, Mr. Austin?"

"I'm not sure yet, Mr. Fairfield. Perhaps in two or three weeks. Keep me posted as to your whereabouts, and I'll find you somehow."

"Do. We are going direct to Rome, and shall stay there for a time before we begin a series of other cities."

"Are you going to Milan?" asked Cadwalader Oram.

"Yes, later," said Mr. Fairfield, and Patty said, "Why?"

"Because I want you to be sure to see the man with his skin hanging over his arm."

"What!"

"Yes, truly. It's a great statue,—in the Cathedral, you know. The gentleman was flayed,—he was one of the noble family of martyrs,—and it was his whim to have his statue taken, with his whole skin flung gracefully over one arm. It's a most impressive sight."

"I should think so!" said Patty. "I'll jot that down in my book. I'm making a list of things to see that are not in the guidebooks."

"Well, you won't find that in a guidebook. But be sure not to miss it."

"We won't," said Mr. Fairfield, "it sounds extremely interesting."

"I'm going to coax mother to let me go," said Flo Carrington. "She's always promised me an Italian trip, and Snippy could take me as well as not."

"Who's Snippy?" asked Patty.

"My governess. She's been with us for years, and she's awfully capable and well-travelled, and languaged, and all that. If she will take me, and mother lets me go, may I see you sometimes?"

"You may, indeed," said Mr. Fairfield, answering for his daughter. "Come right along, Miss Carrington, and we'll be of service to you in any way we can."

"Oh, thank you," said Flo, her dark eyes dancing at the thought of such a pleasure trip. "I'll try to wheedle mumsie into it, and I'll let you know, Patty, if I succeed. I'll write you in London."

"I wish my mumsie would let me go," put in Caddy Oram, in such plaintive tones that they all laughed. "But she can't spare her pet boy at present, so I can only wish you all sorts of happy experiences, Miss Fairfield."

The young man rose to go, and soon there

A Farewell Party

was a general departure of most of the guests. Floyd Austin and Peter Homer tarried after the others had gone, and Lady Hamilton proposed that they all go indoors, for the evening air was growing chill. Then to the dining-room for a bit of a farewell supper, and Patty, as guest of honour, was queen of the merry feast.

"I am very sorry to lose my little Miss Yankee Doodle," said Sir Otho. "Of all the American girls I've ever met,—and I've never met any other,—she's the most like an English girl."

"I'm sorry not to return the compliment," said Patty, "but you're not the least bit like an American. Though you're quite the nicest Englishman I know."

A groan from Mr. Homer and a wail from Floyd Austin greeted this speech.

"Never mind," said Austin, cheerfully, "our own English lassies like us, anyway."

"And mayn't we count on your admiration, Mrs. Fairfield?" said Peter Homer. "I trust all American ladies are not so exclusive in their favours as Miss Patricia."

"You may indeed," said Nan, smiling; "and let me advise you not to take Patty's words too

[55]

literally. I'm beginning to think that since she escaped my restraining influences she has developed coquettish tendencies. I'd not be surprised to learn that she admires both you young men extremely."

"Good for you, Nan!" cried Patty. "I do! I think they're great! and I'm not a coquette at all. I'd like to be, but I don't know how."

"Don't bother to learn," said Peter Homer. "It will come naturally after a while."

"'Deed I won't bother to learn," returned Patty. "I've too much to learn now. I want to learn Italian perfectly, before I start for Italy next week, and I want to learn all about art and architecture, and everything like that, before I go, too."

"Take the same advice for those things," said Austin; "don't bother to learn them, and they'll come naturally after a while."

"I agree to that," said Lady Hamilton. "Patty will learn more of art and architecture by being thus suddenly pushed into it than she could learn from a hundred text-books or tutors."

"Right!" agreed Sir Otho, heartily. "But don't try too hard to learn, little girl; just enjoy. These are your years for enjoying.

[56]

A Farewell Party

When you're my age you'll have time to learn."

"That's a new theory," said Mr. Fairfield, smiling, "but I rather think it's a sound one."

"I think so, too," said Nan. "I know lots of people who have just spoiled a perfectly good trip through Italy, because they learned so hard they had no time to enjoy."

"One should go through Italy," said Mr. Homer, "with a mind like a sieve. Let it alone, and worthless trifles will sift through, and the big, important things will remain."

"All this is very comforting," said Patty, with a relieved sigh; "I had expected to cram as if for an examination, all next week. Now, I shan't even open a book."

"Having supplied Miss Fairfield with all necessary advice and information, the two scholarly and erudite gentlemen rose to take their leave," drawled Austin, as he rose from his chair and beckoned to Mr. Homer to do the same.

Peter Homer made his adieus, and then, saying good-by to Patty, he added:

"I wish I were to show you my Italy, but perhaps it's just as well for you to discover your

[57]

own. Still, I must warn you not to let the glamour gather too thickly. Brush it off once in a while, and look at the real thing."

"I'll remember," promised Patty. "But we'll see you again, sooner or later?"

"Oh, yes; I'll be in Italy before Christmas, and everybody in Italy runs against everybody else, somewhere. Good-by."

"Good-by," said Patty, with a kindly politeness, and turned to say the same to Austin Floyd.

"Be sure to go to the Aquarium in Naples," he reminded her, for the fourteenth time. "The polyps are so pleasantly disgusting, and that fat red starfish is a love. Don't disgrace your country,—remember you're *Murrican*. I shall miss you,—oh, my heart will be as an empty colander! My dolour will be as of one without hope! I shall be as a mullein stalk— but, 'tis better so! Good-by!"

Austin's melodramatic tone was so absurd that the final good-bys were said amid much laughter, but Patty was conscious of a sincere regret at leaving the gay merriment of Markleham Grange, and its pleasant neighbours.

Next morning the three Fairfields started for London.

A Farewell Party

Sir Otho and Lady Kitty partly promised to join them later in Italy, but the matter was not fully decided.

Flo Carrington, too, had sent over an early note, excitedly saying that she was not yet sure she could go, but the outlook was extremely hopeful.

Late in the afternoon they reached London, and as they left the train and found themselves in the ponderous bustle of the railway station, going through the usual distracting hunt for their luggage, Patty's love for the great city came back to her, and she remarked to Nan that she greatly perferred city to country at any time.

"You *are* a chameleon, Patty," said Nan, laughing. " I always said you were. Wherever you are, you immediately claim that it's the best place in the world."

"And a happy disposition, that is," broke in Mr. Fairfield. " Though I'm ready to admit that this sitting on one's trunk, to prevent another citizen from attaching it, is not my idea of luxurious ease."

However, as always finally happens, a porter performed a great magic, and the party, in a cab, drove off to the Savoy. Once again in one of its pleasantest apartments, the dust of travel removed, and tea served, it seemed like getting back home once more.

Mr. Fairfield, having pronounced against a restaurant dinner, had a delightful meal sent up to their own cosy drawing-room, and the three greatly enjoyed their family reunion.

"You people are the best," declared Patty, as she lingered appreciatively over her somewhat scanty portion of ice cream. "By the way," she interrupted herself, "I know why in London they always say 'ice,' instead of 'ice cream.' It's because they never serve enough of it to justify the longer title, though it's of the same materials and quite as good as the American variety. Well, as I was saying, you two are the best people I know. I've had quite enough of friends, and acquaintances, and hostesses, and staying guests, and all that; I'm glad to be back with my relatives."

"I'd think more of that, Patty," said Nan, smiling, "if I weren't sure that you'd take the first chance that offered to go straying off again."

"Isn't she awful, Daddy?" said Patty, placidly. "She doesn't know a compliment when she sees one. Well, let's have these empty

A Farewell Party

plates removed, and get out our maps and plans. I'm crazy to see where we're going."

"We shan't have a cast-iron itinerary," said Mr. Fairfield, as he produced a bundle of maps and time-tables and memoranda. "We'll leave next Wednesday for Paris, stay there a day or two, if you girls want to shop a little, then when we're ready, we'll take the Rome express, right through. After we're well settled in Rome, and have seen more or less of its sights, we'll plan what to do next. In a general way, I may say that we'll go from Rome up to the other principal cities, and back to Rome again. We may decide to spend the whole winter there, but, for my part, I'd be best pleased, that is, if it suits you two, to eat my Christmas dinner in New York City, U. S. A."

"Me too!" cried Patty, her thoughts suddenly rolling in a homesick wave toward her native land.

"Me too!" cried Nan, enthusiastically, but Mr. Fairfield only smiled, and said:

"We won't decide that now; we'll have a fine Italian trip, and it shall be shorter or longer, as suits our pleasure."

"Dear old Daddy," said Patty, "you have the most gumption of anybody I know. I'm so

[61]

glad I picked out a wise father, as well as such a handsome one."

" I wish you had inherited either trait," said Mr. Fairfield, with a mock sigh, and Patty answered him only by a saucy glance.

The few days that intervened between their arrival in London and their departure for Paris were busy ones for Nan and Patty. There was some shopping to be done, but this was hurried through that they might have more time to pay farewell visits to some of their favourite haunts.

" But you must get some dresses, Patty," said Nan, as Patty, declared her intention of spending a day in the picture galleries; " you can't wear garden-party muslin, and chiffon evening gowns on Italian railroads."

" Italians don't have railroads, my ignorant little stepmother; they have railways,—or, more likely they call them by some absurd, unpronounceable name of their own. Well, as I was saying, I'll get dresses in Paris, but if we're really going home from Italy, straight to New York, and not coming back here again, there are some 'loved spots that my infancy knew' in London, to which I simply *must* repair once more!"

A Farewell Party

"All right, girlie; you've only four days left in London, so spend them as you like."

So Patty wandered about as she chose; spending an afternoon in Westminster Abbey, and a morning in the British Museum, and often enjoying a drive in the parks. There were few people whom they knew in London, as most of them were still in their country-places, but the weather was cool and pleasant, and Patty declared she was glad not to be bothered with social engagements.

At last the day came when they must leave for Paris. Trunks were strapped and despatched. Boxes containing various purchases they had made were shipped directly home to New York, and with real tears in her eyes, Patty stood looking out of the hotel window down on the noisy, bustling Strand.

"Cheer up," said Nan, observing her, "we'll come back here some day, if not this year."

"I never thought of that!" exclaimed Patty, as the smiles broke over her face; "why, of course we shall! What a comfort you are, Nan. Why, I shouldn't wonder if we came over every summer, mayn't we?"

"Every other summer, perhaps," said Nan,

[63]

a little absently, for she was attending to some last matters.

"Come, Patty," said her father, "the cab's here. Wave a weeping farewell to your London joys, and turn a smiling face to fresh fields and pastures new."

"All ready, Father," said Patty, cheerily, and in a few moments they were off.

At Victoria station they took the train for Dover, and Patty looked from the window as long as it was possible to get glimpses of the great city they were leaving.

To many people the crossing of the English Channel is not a pleasing experience. Nan frankly confessed that she did not care for it at all; but Patty and her father, being blessed with entire freedom from any physical discomfort in the matter, went aboard the Channel steamer with ancipations of a pleasant trip across. The ideal time to sail away from the Dover cliffs is mid-afternoon, when the sunlight dazzles on the white chalk formations, and the green grass and blue water and the pink tints on the rocks all form a beautiful panorama of the brightest colouring possible.

Patty and her father having done all they could to make Nan as comfortable as possible, they left

A Farewell Party

her at her own request in charge of a kind-mannered stewardess, and returned to the upper deck. Here, in two steamer chairs they sat, and watched England disappear.

As they went on, the intrusive spray dashed up on the deck, and finally onto the travellers themselves.

Patty laughed in glee, for her travelling cloak was of staunch material, and she thought the dashing drops great fun. But as the spray flew higher, the deckmaster brought tarpaulins to wrap about them, and thus protected, the two seafarers enjoyed the rough crossing.

" Isn't it gay! " cried Patty, as a cloud of drops splashed full in her face, making her curly hair curl tighter about her brow.

" Fine! " answered Mr. Fairfield, but he had to scream to make himself heard above the racket of the sea.

As they neared shore, they went below to tidy up for the landing, and found Nan, radiantly smiling, as she awaited them.

" I'm all right now," she announced, " but I shouldn't have been, if I'd been pitching and tossing about in the upper air as you have. Goodness! but you're a sight! Both of you. Can you get wrung out in time to land, do you

[65]

think?" But in a short time Mr. Fairfield and Patty were transformed into dry and correct-looking citizens, and no sign remained of their watery escapade, save the damp curls that clustered around Patty's forehead.

CHAPTER V

DAYS IN PARIS

THE Fairfields spent a few delightful days in Paris. They staid at a large and pleasant hotel, and their rooms looked out upon the Place Vendôme, which was one of Patty's favourite spots in the French capital.

"I own that column," she remarked to her father, as they looked out the window at the great shaft with its spiral decorations.

"Indeed!" said Mr. Fairfield; "given to you by the French people, as a token of regard and esteem?"

"Not exactly that," said Patty. "I own it by right of adoption, or rather, appropriation. All the things I specially like, and that are too big to carry home, I own that way."

"A fine plan," commented her father. "And it has the advantage of being a cheap one too. But you must remember this Vendôme column especially, for you'll see its twin in Rome."

"Another,—just like it?"

[67]

"Not just like it, but similar. The one in Rome is Trajan's Column, and is of marble. But this one, of masonry, covered with plates of bronze, was constructed in imitation of the Roman one. This, however, is nearly twice as high."

"Oh, pooh, then I shan't care for such a little sawed-off thing at all."

"Wait till you see it," said her father, laughing. "I think you'll find it interesting."

"And is Trajan on top of it, as Napoleon is on this?"

"Trajan was, at first. But he has been replaced by a statue of St. Peter."

"I'm glad I'm going to see it," said Patty, contentedly. "I love columns."

"That's right, child. Learn to know columns and arches and steps, and you're fairly started on the road to architecture."

"Steps!" cried Patty, in surprise, "are steps ever beautiful?"

"Yes, indeed. Don't you remember I called your attention to them many times in London. Those of the church of St. Martin's-in-the-Field, for instance."

"Oh, yes, I remember those—I must look up this matter of steps."

"I'll show you plenty in Italy. I'm not going to overburden you, Patty, with instructive lore, but you must acquire a general knowledge of what you're seeing."

"Yes, I want to. I don't want to talk like the people who say, ' I don't know a thing about art, but I know what I like.' "

"If you ever express that sentiment, I'll disown you. Some people invariably like the wrong things."

"Oh, I know how to find out what's worth while. You just pick out a most stupid and uninteresting little picture or statue, and then you look in your Baedeker and he tells you it's the gem of the collection."

"You're hopeless!" declared her father. "I wash my hands of you, and you can do your sightseeing in your own way."

But he well knew she was only jesting, and many a pleasant hour they spent among the art treasures in Paris, while Patty unconsciously absorbed a foundation of true principles of worth and beauty.

The statue of the Venus of Milo was her greatest delight. She never tired of standing in front of it to gaze up into the beautiful face.

"Isn't it strange," she said to her father, one

day, "that the expression of that face should be so exquisite, so,—so,—well, so perfectly lovely that I can't stop looking at it; and yet, all the photographs of it are so different. The photographs all make her have a supercilious, ill-natured air, while the real statue is anything but that."

"I agree with you," said Nan. "I've often noticed it. And the plaster casts, or the bronzes, are not a bit like the original."

"Of course," said Mr. Fairfield, "the plaster or bronze of reduced size can't be expected to be exact portraits, but surely a photograph should give the expression of the original face. For, doubtless, the lady stands still when she has her picture taken."

"But the pictures *aren't* like her," insisted Patty. "I've bought seventeen different photographs of her, including post-cards, and they're not the leastest mite like that dear face."

"Seventeen!" exclaimed Mr. Fairfield; "are you going to set up a shop in New York?"

"No, indeed, but I've been trying to get a satisfactory picture, and I can't."

On their way home Patty asked to stop at a picture shop so she might prove her assertions.

"I'm afraid to go in," said Mr. Fairfield, as she paused at a small shop on the Rue de Rivoli, "you'll buy seventeen more, and expect me to pay for them!"

"No, I won't. Come on in; I know the dealer and he'll show us his wares."

The proprietor of the shop was a funny little old Frenchman, who spoke little English. He recognized Patty, and, shaking his head, said "*Non,* no ones that are new."

"He means he hasn't any new photographs of the Venus, since I was here yesterday," explained Patty, laughing. "But, now, Father, look at these and I'll show you what I mean."

Together, they looked at a number of photographs of the celebrated statue, and suddenly Nan exclaimed; "You're right, Patty! and I know why. It's because all these photographs are taken from too high a level. We look at the face of the Venus from below, it was made to be looked at that way. But all these photographs have been taken by cameras raised to the level of the statue's head, or above it, and that foreshortens her face the wrong way. Why, look, in this one you see all the top of her head. Looking at the real statue, you see only the hair above her brow. I can't explain it exactly, but that's what makes her expression so different."

"It *is*, Nan," cried Patty, "it makes her upper lip curl, and her nose shrink up!"

"Patty, Patty!" said her father, "don't use such expressions. But I believe you're right, Nan, a photograph taken from the same height as our eyes, would give a far different view of the face."

"Yes, indeed," said Patty. "Oh, I wish they'd let me take one."

"They won't," said Mr. Fairfield, "so you'll just have to engrave her on your memory."

Though they were convinced that their theory was right, they couldn't persuade the old Frenchman to agree with them. He admitted that the pictures were unlike the expression of the original face, but he shrugged his shoulders and said;

"Many photographs,—many postcards,—but only one *orichinal!*" And the rapt look in his eyes showed that he, like Patty, preferred his memory of the marble to any possible reproduction of it.

The last day they spent in Paris, Nan declared she was going to buy things.

"We'll do plenty of sightseeing in Italy," she

said, "but there's nothing there to buy, except heads of Dante and models of the Roman Forum."

"And beads," said Patty. "I'm going to get pecks of beads. Everybody expects you to bring them home a string or two."

"All right," said Nan, "but I mean gorgeous raiment. Paris is the only place for that. So, to-day, I buy me some wide-reaching hats, and frippery teagowns and other gewgaws. Want to go, Patsy?"

"'Deed, I do. I adore to buy feathers and frills."

"You're two vain butterflies," said Mr. Fairfield, "but if you'll excuse me from going with you on this excursion, I'll agree to pay the bills you send home."

This was a highly satisfactory arrangement, and the two ladies started out for a round of the shops.

Patty had such good taste, and Nan such good judgment, that they bought only the most desirable things, and a fine collection they made.

"It's really economy to buy these, Patty," said Nan, holding up some embroidered waists as sheer and fine as a handkerchief, "for they're about half the price they cost at home; and as

[73]

these styles are ahead of ours, they'll be all right for next summer."

"Right you are," said Patty, gaily; "and what we don't want ourselves will be lovely for Christmas presents. And, oh, Nan, do look at these lace parasols! I'm going to get one for Marian; she'll be wild over it."

"No, don't, Patty; they are exquisite, and would be just the thing for an English garden party. But Marian would never have an opportunity to carry that fluff of lace and chiffon and pink roses."

"I s'pose not," said Patty, regretfully. "It would look startling to take to the Tea Cub meetings at Vernondale, and she couldn't carry it to New York! Well, I'll leave it, then, and get her a mackintosh or something sensible, instead."

"No, don't go to the other extreme," said Nan, laughing, "get her a hat, if you like, or a feather boa, but get something that the girl can use."

"Sensible little stepmother," said Patty, good-naturedly; "You're aways right, and I'm proud to be your friend and partner."

So the buying went merrily on. Sometimes Patty advised Nan against a combination of colours that didn't quite harmonise, or a decoration that wasn't exactly suitable, and Nan gladly deferred to the younger girl's taste.

"One more farewell glimpse of my Venus, and then I'll go home," said Patty, as the afternoon shadows began to lengthen; and telling the cabman to take them to the Louvre, the two went in for a last sight of the statue.

"*Isn't* she beautiful!" said Patty, for the fiftieth time. "I *know* there'll be nothing in all Italy to compare with her."

"You can't know that till you've been there," said practical Nan, and then she had to drag Patty away, and they went back to the hotel. Their purchases were there awaiting them, so quick are the ways of the Paris shops, and they found Mr. Fairfield in the middle of their sitting room completely surrounded by parcels of all shapes and sizes.

"Snowed under!" he declared, as they came in.

Then he good-naturedly helped to untie the bundles, and pack most of them in trunks to be sent directly to America.

"We want to take whatever luggage we need with us," he said, "but don't take anything we don't need. Excess luggage is expensive in Italy,

[75]

but it's worth the extra expense if we want it for our convenience or pleasure."

So each had a good-sized individual trunk, and another trunk held some evening gowns for Nan and Patty, not to be opened except when social occasions required. Still another trunk held indispensable odds and ends that belonged to all of them, and Mr. Fairfield said that was enough to look after.

"You're lovely people to travel with," said Patty, thoughtfully. "When I came over here with the Farringtons, they had forty-'leven trunks, and they never could find what they wanted without going through the whole lot."

"Much better to get along with a few," said her father, "and then you can find things more easily."

Mr. Fairfield was a systematic and methodical man, and had always instilled these traits into both Patty and Nan. So they were always ready at traintime or a little before, and thus were saved the many annoyances that follow in the train of delay and procrastination.

The next afternoon they started for Rome. Mr. Fairfield chose to go by the " Rome Express " a rapid and well-appointed train. Patty was greatly interested in the strange appoint-

ments of the cars. The Fairfields had two compartments; the larger, double one for the use
of Patty and Nan, the other for Mr. Fairfield.
But at first they all sat together in the double
compartment, which was arranged like a state-
room, and not at all like American sleeping-cars.
They would be on the train two nights and one
day, and Mr. Fairfield chose this plan because it
enabled them to see the Alps by daylight.

"It's just like being in our own house, isn't
it?" said Patty, as they settled their belongings
into place. And indeed it was. Shut away from
the other passengers in their cosy little room,
they were as secluded as if at home. The comfortable seats and convenient little tables, racks
and shelves, made room for all their impedi-
menta, and Patty declared it was lots nicer than
American parlour cars, where everybody was in
the same room.

"Though, of course, you can take a drawing-
room," said Nan.

"Yes, if you're a millionaire," said Patty.
"But this is fixed so everybody can be by themselves."

"Would you rather have your dinner served
in here?" asked her father.

"No; I'd rather go to the dining-car. I want

[77]

to see more of my fellow-travellers. There may be brigands on board. I always think of Italy as peopled with brigands."

"What are they like?" asked Nan, idly.

"Oh, they have big cowboy hats, and red silk sashes, and awful black beards, and they carry cutlasses."

"Those are pirates," suggested her father.

"Oh, yes, so they are. Well, my brigands carry revolvers."

"Oh, no," said Nan, laughing; "not revolvers; you might as well give them tomahawks. Brigands in Italy carry stilettos, of course."

"Stilettos!" cried Patty, in amazement. "They're what you use in embroidery work."

"Well, you *are* an ignorant young person," declared Mr. Fairfield. "An Italian stiletto is a small dagger or poniard."

"Poniard! that's it!" exclaimed Patty. "No well-conducted brigand would carry anything but a poniard. Do you suppose there are many on the train, father?"

"I don't know, I'm sure. But we'll go to dinner now, and if there are any we'll scrape acquaintance with them."

So to the dining-car they went, and Patty cast

discreet but curious glances in at the doors of the other compartments as she passed them.

She saw no brigands, and among the passengers were not many Italians. They all seemed to be people of their own stamp, probably travelling on the same kind of a trip.

The dining-car was comfortable and well-lighted. The tables on one side held four people, and on the other side, each was arranged for two. The Fairfields sat at a quartette table, and as no one occupied the fourth seat, they were pleasantly by themselves again.

It was Patty's first introduction to Italian cookery, and she was much interested in the strange dishes.

The spaghetti, though very good, was served in such large quantities that she was amazed.

" Does anyone ever eat a whole portion? " she said.

But she noticed that many of the diners did do so, and indeed she made large inroads on her own share.

" It's fine! " she said. " I did not know it could be so good."

" On its native heath, spaghetti is quite different from an American arrangement of it," said her father. " I'm glad you like it, for you'll have very few meals without it all the time you're in Italy." The other viands were good, too, and the variety of cheeses and fruits was positively bewildering.

"How different from an English or French meal," said Patty, as they finished. "Isn't it interesting, the different things that different countries eat. Do you suppose that's what makes them the sort of people they are?"

"Your question is a little ambiguous," laughed her father, "but it doesn't always seem logical. For instance, you'd scarcely think this innocent spaghetti would produce a race of ferocious brigands, such as you're expecting to meet. By the way do you see any?"

"Not one," said Patty, as she glanced round the car. "I'm fearfully disappointed."

"Don't give up hope yet. Perhaps they're lying in ambush somewhere, and they'll hold up the train in the night."

After the long dinner, there was not much evening left, so our travellers soon concluded they were ready for their rest.

"Don't be afraid," said Mr. Fairfield, as he left the two ladies, to go to his own sleeping berth. "I don't believe there's a bad-tempered brigand on the train."

"I don't either," said Patty, "so I shan't lie awake in shivering terror."

Soon she and Nan were sleeping quietly in the funny, narrow beds that were so like shelves, and the next thing Patty knew was a knocking at the door of the compartment.

She was awake in an instant and shook the sleeping Nan.

"Wake up," she whispered, "there's a brigand knocking at the door."

"Nonsense!" said Nan, rubbing her eyes, "what do you mean?" The knock was repeated and Nan jumped up.

"What shall we do?" she said. "Perhaps we'd better not answer at all."

But the knocks became more peremptory, and throwing on a kimono, Nan went to the door, and without opening it, said, "Who's there?"

"Open the door," said a commanding voice.

"It *is* a brigand!" said Patty, hopping about on one foot. "Where are your jewels, Nan?"

"Your father has them. Don't be silly, Patty; of course it isn't a brigand, but who can it be? Perhaps Fred is ill."

As the knocking continued, and as the voice kept on demanding that the door be opened,

Nan opened it cautiously and saw before her a big burly man in an official uniform.

"Sorry to disturb you, ma'am," he said, "but have you any luggage in your room?"

"No," said Nan, "only hand luggage."

"How many trunks in the luggage-car?" he went on, and Nan told him.

"Anything dutiable in them?"

"Why, I don't know. What is dutiable?"

"Spirits or tobacco, ma'am."

"Why, no! Of course we haven't any of those things in our trunks."

"Any matches?"

"No."

"Thank you. Good night, madam. Sorry to trouble you."

The big man went away, and Patty tumbled back to bed, murmuring:

"Huh, to be waked up and bothered, and then not see a brigand after all! I do think the customs men might at least wear red silk sashes. They'd be so much more picturesque. What a queer time for him to come to see about the trunks."

"I believe they always come when we cross the border," said Nan, sleepily. "Good-night."

"Good-night," said Patty.

CHAPTER VI

THE GRANDEUR THAT WAS ROME

IT was very early in the morning when the train pulled into the station at Rome. Patty had been up and dressed for some time, watching from the window the strange views and novel sights.

"Here we are," said Mr. Fairfield, and Patty hurried from the train in her eager interest to see the real Rome outside of a map or guide-book.

"Well!" she said, as she found herself in a great station, not so very unlike railroad stations in other countries, "Well! if you call this picturesque, I don't!"

"Nothing can be picturesque when you're hungry," said Nan, "and I'm going to get my breakfast before I express my opinion of the Eternal City."

"Good girl, Nan!" said Mr. Fairfield, approvingly. "And I fancy Patty, too, is ready for some Roman breakfast food."

[83]

"I am hungry," said Patty, "but I'm so surprised at this place! Why!" she went on, as they emerged into the great square in front of the station, "look at the trolley-cars! It's just like New York!"

"You needn't get in a trolley-car," said Mr. Fairfield, laughing at Patty's dismayed expression; "here's the omnibus that's to take us to our hotel. Hop in."

"Pooh! an omnibus!" said Patty, "that isn't appropriate to Rome, either!"

"I know what you want to ride in," said her father. "One of those Roman chariots drawn by four horses, that they race round the ring in, at the circus."

"Those rattlety-bang things?" said Patty, laughing at the recollection. "Yes, they would be all right, only there's so much danger of spilling out behind."

But she climbed into the omnibus with the others and in less than five minutes they were round the corner, and stopping at their own hotel. Mr. Fairfield had selected the Quirinal, as a comfortable and convenient home for them, and when Patty went in, and saw the handsomely appointed halls and picturesque winter-garden, she said, "This is better than

[84]

trolley-cars, but it isn't so very Roman, after all."

"You may as well get rid of your ideas of ancient Rome," said Mr. Fairfield. "There is a little of that left, but most of the Rome you'll have to do with is decidedly twentieth century, and very much up-to-date."

"I believe you!" said Patty, as she noticed the fashionably attired ladies about, and the modern appliances everywhere.

Then they were taken to their rooms, and Patty exclaimed with delight at the pleasant apartment reserved for them.

"At last I've found something different," she cried. "This isn't a bit like our apartments in London or Paris. Oh, Nan, do see this gorgeous gold furniture in our drawing-room! I'm sure the Queen has lent it for our use while we're here!"

"Grand, but stuffy," declared Nan, as she threw off her travelling cloak.

"I like it," said Patty; "it's the first effect of Roman luxury I've seen. Do we lie on couches to eat, father?"

"You may if you like, my dear; though I believe it isn't done much this year, in the best circles."

Patty's Pleasure Trip

Patty went on exploring, and was greatly pleased with the novelty of her new surroundings. There was a grand drawing-room, furnished with heavy velvet hangings and carpets; massive furniture, carved, gilded and upholstered in rich brocatelles; immense crystal chandeliers; elaborate mirrors, pictures and bric-à-brac; and a profusion of palms, statuettes, footstools and sofa pillows.

From this opened a small breakfast-room, also lavishly decorated and furnished. The bedrooms, dressing-rooms, and baths were all in harmonious style, and after a tour of the rooms, Patty declared herself quite satisfied with the modern Roman notions of living.

"And only think," said Mr. Fairfield, "the price we pay for all this gorgeousness is not so much as we paid for far simpler accommodations in Paris or London either."

"Oh, let's live in Rome always, then," cried Patty, enthusiastically, "I love it already."

"Goose-girl!" exclaimed Nan, laughing at her raptures; "go and freshen yourself up, get into a comfortable gown, and then we'll have some breakfast."

Half an hour later the family gathered in

their own breakfast-room, and a delightful meal was served them there.

Patty and Nan, in pretty house dresses, welcomed the delicious fruits and daintily-cooked eggs, and the coffee was pronounced better than that of Paris.

"And as to London," said Nan, "they spell coffee, T, e, a."

"So they do," said Patty, with a wry face at the recollection of London coffee. "Give me Rome, every time!"

"There's this difference, too," said Mr. Fairfield, "you girls will have to readjust your mode of living a little. In Paris, nobody gets around till noon, and then they call luncheon breakfast. While here, people get up and out fairly early, in order to utilize the morning hours, which are the best of the day. Then they come back and stay indoors during the middle of the day; luncheon is promptly at twelve, for that reason; and stay in the house till three or four o'clock, then go out again if you like for the sunset hours."

"How funny!" said Patty. "Luncheon at twelve is very early."

"When you're in Rome you must do as the Romans do," said her father, "and now I've told

[87]

you what that is. But to-day, you two are not going out at all, at least not until four o'clock this afternoon. You must rest this morning, and then, at four, I'll take you out for a drive. We're not going to do a lot of sightseeing in a rush, and get all tired out. We're here for pleasure, and we must take it slowly, or we can't really enjoy it."

"I'm agreeable," declared Patty. "I can spend the day beautifully, unpacking my trunk, and wandering about this hotel, and taking a nap, and chattering with my stepmother, and lots of things. What are you going to do, Daddy?"

"I'm going out to engage a Roman chariot for you to ride about in, and to have the trolley-cars stopped, and the railroad station made over on a more antique plan."

"Oh, don't bother about the station. I shan't need it again till I go home, so let it remain as it is."

"Very well, then; now you two be ready when I come back at noon, and we'll lunch down-stairs."

Mr. Fairfield went away, and Patty and Nan went to their work of unpacking.

Patty was of an orderly nature, and really enjoyed putting her things neatly away in the wardrobes and drawers, of which there were plenty. She was accustomed to wait on herself, and so declined the offers of help from the willing but unintelligible maid who spoke no English.

"I suppose you're offering to help me," said Patty, smiling at her, "but I can't speak Italian, and I'd rather do things myself anyway."

The little maid did not quite understand the words, but she gathered Patty's meaning, and tripped away to make similar offers to Nan. Nan couldn't talk Italian either, but she was inclined to have help, so, by the aid of smiles and gestures, she quite made herself understood and her rooms were soon in order.

"What a mess!" she exclaimed, as a couple of hours later she went to Patty's room and found that young woman in the midst of a sea of dresses, hats, slippers, and toilet accessories of all sorts.

"A lovely mess," returned Patty, placidly. "I'll soon straighten it out. But I never could do it, with a Choctaw-speaking Roman trying to jabber out help."

"Lucretia isn't Choctaw; we understood each

other perfectly, without words, and she's an awfully well-trained maid."

"Is her name Lucretia? Is she of the old Borgia crowd? Now, she'll murder us in our sleep!"

"Like your brigand did! Patty, you'll never get these clothes put away. I'll help you."

So, working together, the room was soon tidy, and Patty had the satisfaction of knowing that all her belongings were put away in proper order.

"I like them so I can put my hand on anything I want in the dark," she said to Nan. "Though, indeed, it's rarely I want my books or sewing materials in the dark. Or my best hat, for that matter. What would be the use of one's best hat in the dark? Nobody could see it!"

But she easily found the clothes she did want, and when Mr. Fairfield returned, he found two very correct looking ladies, in fresh white costumes, ready to go to luncheon with him.

"I've good news for you," he said, after they were seated at table; "I ran across Jim Leland, and he's living here in Rome, and he proposes to make it pleasant for us in lots of ways while we're here."

[90]

"That's lovely," said Nan; "it's always pleasant to know somebody who lives in a place. Who's he, Fred?"

"I used to know him twenty years ago, but haven't seen him since. He's a bachelor, and has the reputation of being somewhat of a recluse, but I know he'll be genial and hospitable where we're concerned. He and I are good chums, though we don't meet often. He has asked us to dine with him some night, and I've accepted for us all on Monday. I suppose you've no other engagement, Patty?"

"Not unless the King asks me informally to dinner," she replied. "Where does Mr. Leland live?"

"Not far away. Just across the street, in fact. He has bachelor apartments, where he has lived for years, I believe."

They lingered over their pleasant luncheon, and then strolled out to the beautiful garden at the back of the hotel.

Here there were no flowers, but palms and strange tropical plants in great variety. So dense was the foliage in some places that Patty called it a jungle, and appropriating a wicker chair, declared her intention of remaining there to read for a while.

"Do as you choose until four," said her father, "and then your Roman chariot will await you."

The Roman chariot proved to be a low, comfortable open carriage, that Mr. Fairfield had engaged to be at their disposal during their whole stay in Rome.

As they started off on their first drive round the city, Patty asked where they were going.

"Not to many places to-day," said her father. "Just a drive to the Pincio, and to get a bird's-eye view of the city. But keep your eyes open, for this drive will always remain in your memory."

And it did. Patty never forgot that first afternoon in Rome. She almost held her breath as they drove rather slowly along the streets, and her ideas formed and changed and fled so swiftly that she scarcely could be said to have any.

Her conversation was limited to gasps of surprise and delight, exclamations of awe and wonder, and little squeals of glee and merriment.

At last she recognised one thing at least, and cried out, "Oh, isn't that Trajan's Column? It's just like the Column Vendôme."

"Good for you," said her father, " to recognise it. Yes, that's it, and next to it you may see Trajan's Forum."

"Not a very big one," said Patty, a little disappointed, "but very tidy and set in neat rows."

"Well, the columns weren't just like that to begin with," said Mr. Fairfield, "but they've been set up in straight rows since."

They went on for some distance, and then, at a word from Mr. Fairfield, the driver paused and stopped at a point that commanded a fine view of the Coliseum.

Patty first sat and looked at it. Indeed, they all sat silent, looking at the great structure, as its wonderful lines stood out against the blue sky.

"I didn't think it was like that," said Patty, at last. "I've seen pictures of it, but, well, I don't think it takes a good picture!"

"No, it doesn't," agreed Mr. Fairfield. "No photograph or painting of the Coliseum can give the least idea of the calm sublimity of the building itself."

They drove round it, Patty becoming more and more deeply interested at every step; but Mr. Fairfield said they would not go inside that day, as he had other plans.

So they went on, under the great arch of Constantine, and at this Patty was again dumb with awed admiration.

"How big the things are," she said.

"And how old," added Nan, greatly impressed with the ancient monuments.

Then they drove round by the Roman Forum. This was altogether too much, and she gazed at it, with such a helpless expression on her face that Mr. Fairfield laughed at her.

"Drive on," he said to the man; "we'll see the Forum some other time. Well, Patty, my child, is Rome antique enough, or is it all trolley-cars and railroad stations?"

"Oh, Father," said Patty, and because of a queer lump in her throat, she couldn't talk in her usual merry fashion.

"There, there, dearie, don't take it too seriously. I want you to love it all, but don't let it break you up so."

"I can't help it," said Patty, laughing as she wiped her eyes with her handkerchief; "it's so big,—so—so——"

"So overpowering,—yes, I know. But that's why I want you to get used to it by degrees. Now, we'll go through some beautiful gardens, and on to the Pincio."

Away they went along the Corso Umberto,

[94]

The Grandeur That Was Rome

and passed many statues, villas, buildings, fountains, and arches, but none of them so impressed Patty as the ancient ruins had done.

"Why is it," she asked her father, "that the ruins are so much more impressive than the complete buildings?"

"That's partly glamour," he said, with a twinkle in his eye, for he remembered what Patty had told him of Mr. Homer's remarks on glamour.

"And partly what else?" she asked.

"Partly the grandeur of the monuments themselves. If you hadn't been affected at the sight of the Coliseum I should have packed you back to New York by the first boat."

"And I should have deserved to go," said Patty, decidedly. "I give you both fair warning,—the first thing I do every morning while I'm in Rome is to go straight to the Coliseum and hug it. After that I'll go to see the other sights."

"Can you reach all the way around it?" asked Nan, smiling.

"Don't be too literal," said Patty, smiling back. "I shall only hug it figuratively, but, oh, I do love it! The Venus of Milo has a rival in my affections. No, not a rival, ex-

[95]

actly, for they're too different to be compared. But they're both my favourite statues."

"That's one way to put it," laughed her father. "But here we are on the top of the Pincian Hill. Will you get out and have some cakes and ices?"

They did so, and Patty found it delightful to sit at one of the little tables under the trees, and have a Roman afternoon tea. There were a great many people about, some of whom looked like Americans, and Patty noticed two or three who belonged in their own hotel.

"Shall we get acquainted with any of the people at the hotel?" she asked.

"Yes, I think so," Nan answered. "There are some people from Philadelphia there, whom I know slightly. I think I'll look them up to-morrow."

"Oh, of course we'll make acquaintances, sooner or later," said Mr. Fairfield.

"The Coliseum is chum enough for me," said Patty, with a dreamy look. "I don't care for anybody else."

"Glamour has hit you hard," said her father; "we'd better be going home and give you a change of scene."

[96]

CHAPTER VII

AMERICAN FRIENDS AND OTHERS

"SHE'S coming!" announced Patty, as the family sat at luncheon some days later.

"Who's coming?" asked Nan, looking up from her own letters. They were all reading their mail, which usually arrived about midday.

"Why, Flo Carrington, and her governess, whom she always calls 'Snippy.' I don't know what the lady's real name is."

"Good!" said Mr. Fairfield. "I'll be glad for you to have a young companion, and Madame Snippy can probably look after you both."

"Or Flo and I can look after her," observed Patty. "I've never met the lady, but I think she goes around with her nose in a book. I've always heard of her widespread knowledge of all sorts."

"That will be a good thing for you," said her father. "You're not overburdened with book-

[97]

lore, and though this is a pleasure trip for you, I hope you'll acquire some information that will stay by you."

"There's one thing sure," said Patty; "as soon as I get home, I'm going to take up a course of Roman history. It never seemed interesting to me before, but now I know I shall like it."

"I'm with you," said Nan. "We'll be a class all by ourselves, and read every morning, after we're back in New York."

"And then, you see, Father," went on Patty, "I can remember all these things I'm seeing now, and, before you know it, I'll be a great scholar."

"I'm not alarmed at the idea of your becoming a blue-stocking. Indeed, I doubt if your interest remains after you've left these actual scenes."

"Oh, yes, it will! I want to study up all about the early Christian martyrs and the cruel emperors. I'm sure it will be most interesting. You see, Flo knows it all. She has all history at her tongue's end. And she knows all about the great works of art and everything."

"Can she recite the names of the twelve ' world-pictures ' ? " asked Nan, smiling.

American Friends and Others

"Oh, she doesn't know it that way! No 'Half Hours with the Best Artists,' for hers! She really knows, and she's so unostentatious about it."

"Then she'll be a good chum for you. Are they coming here? And when?"

"Yes, Father. They've engaged rooms here, on the same floor as ours, and they'll arrive next week. Oh, I'm so glad. I can go around a lot with them, and that will leave you and Nan to flock by yourselves. Won't you be lonesome?"

"If we are, we'll tag after you," said Nan. "Patty, I think that I'll introduce ourselves to those people over there. They're the Van Winkles from Philadelphia, and I met Mrs. Van Winkle some years ago, though she may not remember me. But I think she does, for she has smiled pleasantly two or three times."

"All right, Nan. I'll go with you. Let's go right after luncheon, if they stop in the winter-garden, as they probably will. Daddy can make himself invisible behind a newspaper until we call him into the game."

So, as they rose from the table and passed through the winter-garden, which was also a favourite lounging-place at all seasons of the

[99]

year, they found the Van Winkles had paused there, and were having their coffee at a small table.

Nan soon discovered that Mrs. Van Winkle did indeed remember her, and that they were all glad to become better acquainted. Mr. Fairfield was summoned to join the group, and a pleasant hour followed. The Van Winkle family consisted of the father and mother, also a son and daughter. Patty liked the young people, and was much amused to learn that the young man, whom his sister called Lank, was really named Lancaster. The girl's name was Violet, and she explained that she chose it herself because it went so well with Van Winkle.

"I really had no name until I was about ten," she said. "They always called me Birdie or Tottie, or some foolish pet name. But I liked Violet, so I just took it."

"It's a pretty name," said Patty, with amiable intent, "and Lancaster is a pretty name, too."

"Yes," said Violet, "but we call him Lank, because he's so fat and stuffy."

He was a stout young man, and of a very good-natured countenance. He seemed to admire Patty, and soon they all fell into easy conversation.

"Have you been here long?" asked Patty.

"Nearly a month," said Violet. "We were thinking of going on next week, but now that we've met you I'd like to stay longer."

"I hope you will," said Patty, cordially. "I've a friend coming in a few days, and I know we could all have a good time together. I love a lot of people, don't you?"

"I do, if they pull together," said Lank. "But if you start out sight-seeing with a bunch of people, they never all want to go to the same place at the same time."

"I suppose that's so," said Patty, "but I've only my father and mother in my party at present, and we go together, of course. But I've not seen much yet. We've only been here a few days, and I've spent most of the time in the Coliseum and Roman Forum. I do love them so, and I go there expecting to study out the ruins and columns, and then I forget all about studying, and just wander about, thinking of the old Romans who used to be there."

"That's what I do!" exclaimed Lank. "I'm mad about the Forum, and I just shuffle around it with my tongue out, sort of lapping it up."

"He does!" said Violet, laughing. "You ought to see him. He looks like an idiot."

" I'd rather look like an idiot than a tourist,"
said Lancaster, a little resentfully.

" Don't worry," said Patty. " I'm sure you
don't look the least like a tourist. I know you
don't keep one forefinger stuck into a Baedeker,
and the other pointing."

" No, I don't. But," and the boy's eyes
twinkled, " I carry a pack of postcards instead
of a Baedeker! "

" Good for you! " cried Patty. " I love postcards too."

" They're so useful," said Violet, " to direct
your cabman where to go. The cabmen never talk
English, but if you show a postcard, they take you
right to the place. Go out with us to-morrow,
won't you, and let's visit the Forum together? "

" Indeed I will," said Patty, " I'd love to.
But I suppose I must start in on the churches
pretty soon. I'll admire them, I expect, but I
know they won't take hold of me as the
ruins do."

" So the ruins have caught you, have they? "
said a deep voice behind Patty's chair, and
turning quickly, she saw Peter Homer, smiling
down at her.

" Mr. Homer! " she cried, delightedly, as she
jumped up to greet him.

"I told you I'd appear sooner or later," he said, smiling at her surprise.

"And I'm glad you came as soon as you did!" she replied merrily, and then she introduced him to the Van Winkles, and Mr. and Mrs. Fairfield added their welcome.

"I'm just here on one of my wonder-wanders," said Mr. Homer, by way of explaining his sudden appearance. "Every few years I run down to Rome, and wander about, wondering. It's a most satisfying occupation, and I never tire of it."

"That's a good expression," said Patty, thoughtfully. "I believe I'd rather wander around and wonder, than to know it all."

"It's a whole lot easier," said Lank Van Winkle. "Let's you out of a lot of study."

"And gives you equally good results," said Mr. Homer. "A short cut and a merry one, is my creed, to knowledge or across a street, or wherever possible."

"You don't seem to pursue that plan in your twenty-volume book," said Patty, smiling.

"Oh, my book? That's intended for other people, so I can't consult my own inclinations in the matter. But when I'm away on my wanderings and wonderings, I try to forget those twenty volumes, and pretend I'm entirely care-free."

"That's right," said Mr. Van Winkle, approvingly; "when you take a vacation, take it thoroughly. That's what I'm doing. I've forgotten that I have a business office in the United States, and I've become, temporarily, a Roman citizen. Are you staying at this hotel, Mr. Homer?"

"No; my fate decrees an humbler home. But I'm comfortably housed only a few blocks away, and I shall hope to see you all again. Now, I must pursue my wanderings, as I have an engagement shortly. By the way, Miss Fairfield, did you know your friend Floyd Austin is on his way here?"

"Really?" said Patty; "how delightful. We can have a Roman reunion, for Miss Carrington is coming too."

"Yes, I know it. And Caddy Oram is with Austin. We must have a meeting of the clan soon."

"We will," said Patty; "I'll invite you all to tea as soon as Flo arrives, and we'll have a lovely time."

"Don't you always have a lovely time?" asked Peter Homer, as he said good-by to Patty.

[104]

"Yes, indeed," she replied. "And in Rome, who could help it?"

"No one with eyes," he said; "and which has pleased you more, so far, the glamour or the ruins?"

Patty thought a moment.

"I can't distinguish them," she said, at last. "They're so mixed up with each other, and both so wonderful."

Mr. Homer smiled. "That's as it should be," he said. "But if I may, I'd like to wonder a little with you. What are you doing to-morrow morning?"

"Going to the Forum with the two Van Winkles," answered Patty. "Won't you go with us?"

"I'll be glad to. Suppose I meet you here at ten o'clock."

"Do. That will be fine. I've only just met the Van Winkles, but I like them already."

"Yes, they're attractive people," said Mr. Homer, a little absently, and then he went away.

Although Peter Homer was only about twenty-five, and the Van Winkles were near Patty's age, he seemed much older than the other three. Patty realised this, and attributed it to his really serious and scholarly nature, which he hid behind his pretence of taking everything lightly. She liked the man very much, for he was most interesting and amusing, but he sometimes had a preoccupied air which made Patty feel young and ignorant.

"Well, he can go with us to-morrow," she thought, "and if he thinks we're not wise enough for him, he needn't go again."

It was the evening they were to dine at Mr. Leland's, and Patty looked forward with pleasure to a visit to a real Roman home.

"Of course," she said to Nan, "I don't mean ancient Roman. I've learned better than to look for couches instead of dining chairs; but I think it will be fun to see how an American lives in Rome."

So Patty ran away to her room to dress for the dinner party.

She chose a white chiffon, with a round, low-cut neck, and a skirt that billowed into soft frills, and to it she added a beautiful Roman sash that she had bought that very day.

She was peacocking up and down in front of the long mirror, when Nan came in.

"I suppose I'm too grown up to wear a Roman sash," said Patty, looking over her shoulder at the soft silk ends, with their knotted fringe; "but the colours are so lovely, and it seems appropriate."

"By all means wear it, if you like," said Nan; "it's a beautiful one; and anyway, I don't suppose Mr. Leland will know a sash from a redingote."

Patty laughed at this, and concluded to wear her sash.

"You'll be wasted on him, then," she added, "for you do look bewitching in that mauve tulle."

Nan did look lovely in her pretty evening gown, and Mr. Fairfield had reason to feel proud of the two distinguished-looking ladies he escorted downstairs.

"Don't bother with that ridiculous elevator," said Patty, as she led the way to the staircase. "I think its rheumatism is bad to-day. It grunts fearfully, and limps like everything."

"It never seems well on Mondays," said Nan, sympathetically. "I think it's overworked, poor thing."

"Overworked!" put in Mr. Fairfield; "it makes about three round trips each day."

"I like better to walk down, anyway," said Patty. "These staircases are so red velvety, and white marble-y, and gold-banister-y." And with a hop, skip, and jump, she landed on the lower hall floor.

" Behave yourself, Patty," admonished Nan. " Don't jump around like an infant, even if you are wearing a little girl's sash."

" I've learned," said Patty, with an air of great wisdom, " that an American young woman in Rome may do anything she chooses, and she is excused just because she's *Murrican.*"

" Don't you believe it," said her father. " You behave yourself properly, or you can't go dining out with your elders again."

" Then you can't go," cried irrepressible Patty, " for you can't leave me alone, either ! "

But Patty's manners were really above reproach, and it was a most correctly behaved American girl who entered Mr. Leland's drawing-room. That gentleman proved to be a man of about Mr. Fairfield's age, and he was delighted to welcome guests from his native land.

" To humour my health," he said, " I have lived in Rome for many years, but my heart is still true to the old flag, and I wish I might go back and live beneath its red, white, and blue."

" But wouldn't you hate to give up all this splendour ? " asked Patty, glancing about at the unusually fine apartment.

[108]

"Yes and no," replied Mr. Leland, smiling. "I've collected my household gods with great care, and they wouldn't bear transplanting to America, but still my native heath calls loudly to me at times."

"Why couldn't you take all these beautiful things home with you?" asked Nan.

"I could; but they wouldn't feel at home in an American house. Imagine these rooms transported bodily to New York. They would appear bizarre and over-ornate, while here they are neither."

"That's one reason I love Rome," said Patty, enthusiastically; "it's all red velvet, and carved gold frames, and marble filigree-work, and heavy tapestries, and mosaic floors,—oh, I adore it!"

"You've a barbaric love of colour," said Mr. Leland, smiling, "unusual in a young American girl. But you must remember that all this colour and gilding is only right under the blue and gold of the Italian sky. In New York it would be a jarring note."

Patty sighed unconsciously, for she began to realise there was a great deal to know, of which she was entirely ignorant.

"Don't take it too seriously, child," said Mr.

Leland, reading her thought. "Remember I've spent twenty years learning these things, and you've not even begun yet. I'm sure your natural instincts are fairly true; all you need is instruction and experience. Have you seen St. Peter's?"

"Yes," said Patty, "but I've only bowed to it. I haven't shaken hands with it yet. But I know one thing about it. Somebody told me. It's *baroque*."

Mr. Leland smiled, and said, not at all unkindly:

"Whoever told you that was utterly ignorant of the real meaning of *baroque*. In no sense does it apply to St. Peter's. That church, my dear child, if anybody asks you, is flubdubby."

"Is what?" exclaimed Patty.

"Flubdubby in the extreme. I may say it's pure flubdub. If you want to impress any one with your knowledge of architecture, say that, and you'll hit the nail on the head."

Patty was almost afraid her host was making fun of her, but his earnest manner proved he was not.

"We won't go into details, now," he said, "but some day I'll take you there, and show you what I mean."

Dinner was served then, and Patty went into a dining-room that made her feel as if she had been transplanted to China itself. It was really a remarkable room. The walls were hung with marvellous satin embroideries that had belonged to the Empress Dowager of China; and the screens and chairs were covered with the same exquisite handiwork. Bronzes and pottery of rare values were everywhere, and all of the dinner service was of porcelain, silver, and gold, that had once graced the tables in royal palaces.

Patty was so enraptured, looking at the beautiful and curious things, she had no appetite for the viands that were offered her by soft-footed, swift-motioned Celestials.

" You are more susceptible to beauty and colour than any one I ever saw, Miss Fairfield," said her host, after he had covertly watched Patty's shining eyes.

" She is," declared her father. " From a child she has loved pretty things, and she has a perfect passion for bright colour."

" But always with a good sense of colour values," put in Nan, lest Mr. Leland should think Patty a little barbarian.

" I'm sure of that," he said, kindly; " and I shall hope, Miss Fairfield, to have the pleasure of showing you some of the most beautiful things in Rome, which are not shown, except to appreciative eyes.''

Patty's appreciative eyes danced at this, for she knew Mr. Leland was a man of influence, and could take her to many places where strangers were not usually allowed.

After dinner a delightful evening was spent viewing the treasures collected by their host on his many trips to Oriental countries, and Patty became more and more awed at his extensive knowledge of the art works of all ages and countries.

" I don't see how you remember it all," she said, looking at him earnestly. " I should think you'd have to have a head as big as the Coliseum, and,—you haven't ! "

" No one can have the ' big head,' " said Mr. Leland, smiling, " when he realises the great minds and great geniuses who have produced these wonderful things."

" No," said Patty, " and I can't even appreciate it. I can only wonder."

CHAPTER VIII

PLAYING HOUSE

IT was a merry party of four that started off next morning to visit the Roman Forum.

In the spacious, open carriage Patty and Violet sat facing Lancaster and Mr. Homer, and they drove slowly through the streets of Rome, remarking their favourite points of interest on either side.

"First, let's go and hug the Coliseum," said Patty, so they went in that direction.

"Want to go in?" asked Peter Homer, as they approached the entrance.

"No, not to-day," said Patty. "I'll just give it a good squeeze, so it will know I haven't forgotten it."

Patty spread her arms toward the great structure, her blue eyes filled with loving affection.

"I hope your somewhat dilapidated friend appreciates your devotion," remarked Peter, smiling at Patty's fervour.

[113]

"It isn't dilapidated!" she retorted. "It has only just reached perfection."

"The perfection of old age," said Violet. "I love it, too, but I'm not as idiotic about it as Patty. I see its defects."

"I don't," insisted Patty, stoutly, "for it hasn't any."

"Good for you," cried Lank. "That's true loyalty, not to see the imperfections of your friends, whether they have any or not. But here's the Forum, fairly running to meet us."

"Oh, isn't it great!" exclaimed Patty, as she looked eagerly at the picturesque ruins standing out sharply against the blue Italian sky.

"What was the Forum for, in the first place?" asked Violet.

"In earliest times it was a market-place," said Peter, "but later——"

"Oh," broke in the irrepressible Patty, "then, I suppose, this little Roman went to market, this little Roman staid home."

"But no little Roman had roast beef," said Lank. "At least, I suppose they might have done so, but it doesn't seem appropriate."

"They had it, I'm sure," said Violet, "but under a different name. Didn't they, Mr. Homer?"

Playing House

"Probably. They seemed to have everything that was good to eat,—and some things that weren't."

As the party intended to spend the whole morning in the Forum, they dismissed their cab at the entrance.

"Now," said Peter Homer, as they went down among the ruins, "we won't have any maps or guidebooks, we'll just wander around and wonder."

"But you know what all the ruins are, don't you?" asked Patty.

"Oh, yes; I know the names of the temples and things. I'll tell you those as we come to them. This noble collection of pedestals was once the Basilica Julia."

"Let's play house," said Patty, promptly. "I'll be Julia, and live here. I'd love to be a Roman matron."

"But the Julia in question wasn't a Roman matron," said Peter; "in fact, this basilica was named in honour of Mr. Julius Cæsar."

"Oh," said Patty, "and they called him Julia as a pet name, I suppose. How sweet of them!"

"We can play house just the same," said Violet. "I'll live in the temple of Saturn; it's

[115]

roomy and well ventilated. What do you choose, Mr. Homer?"

"I'll live under the arch of Septimius Severus. It's not so large, but it's roofed in case of rain."

"The Temple of Vespasian," for mine," said Lank. "It isn't in very good repair, but perhaps the landlord will fix it up; and anyway, I'll be near sister, if she wants me."

And so these four ridiculous young people went to their chosen abodes.

Patty surveyed the wide expanse of her house with satisfaction, and then taking a pack of postcards from her bag, proceeded to identify the different monuments.

Soon Violet came flying over. "How do you do, Madame Julia?" she said. "Is the Honorable Cæsar at home?"

"No," said Patty, rising with great dignity, and bowing to her guest. "He had to go to market,—to the Forum, I mean. It's his day to make a speech to the Senate or something."

"I've brought my cards," said Violet, dropping back into a modern American mood. "Don't you get the columns mixed up?"

"Yes, I do," said Patty. "But I don't care much. You can wonder better, if you're not sure of your facts."

"Of course you can," said Homer, who, with young Van Winkle, came just then within hearing of the two girls. "Pardon my interruption, Madame Julia, but I've brought a Roman Senator to call on you. Allow me to present Augustus Van Winkleinus, from the ancient City of Philadelphia."

"Ha," said Patty, "methinks we have met aforetime. Art not Lankius the Rotund?"

"I art not!" declared Lank, "I art but a stripling youth."

"A good-natured one, forsooth," said Patty, laughing.

"Good nature, but bad art," said Violet. "Peterus Homerus, what is the noble building next us, with its three columns left standing?"

"I know," cried Patty, "it's the Temple of Castor and Pollux."

"Don't call it that," said Mr. Homer. "Just say the Temple of Castor. It sounds better to trained ears."

"All right, I will," said Patty. "What was it for, anyway?"

"For various commercial uses. Indeed, it was a sort of an office building at one time. It contained the testing-office for weights and meas-

[117]

ures. But that doesn't add to its interest. Just look at the blue sky between those perfect columns, and let that be your only memory of the Temple of Castor."

"Isn't it strange," said Patty, reminiscently, "you said you wished you could show me Italy in your own way, and here you are doing it!"

"Yes, and I'm glad I have the opportunity. How do you like my way?"

"I love it," said Patty. "But all ways lead to Rome, so I suppose that's how you happened to get here just now."

"I suppose so," returned Homer. "But Senator Lancastrius Van Winkleius and I came over to invite you Roman matrons to dine with us in my Triumphal Arch. Will you come?"

"What have you to dine on?" asked Violet.

"Ah, that's the triumph! You come and see. It isn't correct to ask your host such a question."

So the four proceeded to the Arch of Severus, and there on some stones they found a box of sandwiches and a small pile of fruit.

"Primitive service, but good food," remarked Peter, and the girls suddenly realised that they had a fine twentieth-century appetite.

"This is great," declared Patty, as she sat on an old block of marble, with a sandwich in one hand and a bunch of grapes in the other. "I approve of your method of 'seeing Italy,' and I think a triumphal arch the best place in the world to eat sandwiches."

"And then you see," said Peter, "it fixes this particular arch in your mind; and when wiseacres speak of Septimius Severus, you can say to yourself, 'Ah, yes, his is the Arch of the Sandwiches.'"

"I shall never forget it," said Violet, helping herself to some fruit. "I feel a personal friendship for old Severus."

"Incidentally," went on Peter, "you may as well fasten in your memory the facts that this arch was built about 200 A.D., in commemoration of the victorious wars of our friend Severus. These not very beautiful sculpturings represent his soldiers, but as art had begun to decline when these figures were cut, you needn't bother about them much."

"I think they're rather nice," said Patty, examining the multitudinous small figures in basrelief, "but I'm glad I haven't to learn all their names, for there are so many more attractive sculptures."

"There are indeed. But I want you to remember the arch as a whole. And now that you've eaten every last crumb, step outside, and take a look at the beautiful thing."

The quartette lined up, facing the arch, and Peter pointed out its special points of beauty and excellence.

"Where is there another arch, very similar to this?" he asked, at length, and his three hearers tried to think.

"I know!" said Patty, her eyes shining, "it's in Paris. Not the Arc de Triomphe, that has only one front door,—but the other, the Arc du Carrousel!"

"Right you are," said Peter, approvingly. "The Arc du Carrousel was modelled after this one. Remember that, when you have a remembering fit."

"But the Carrousel one has a flight of horses on top," said Patty.

"Right again, my acute observer. However, Mr. Severus once had six fine horses and a chariot on top of this one. Also a statue of himself and his two sons. So, you see, it's a bit of a ruin after all."

"It is so," said Violet. "So much so that, until now, I've liked the Arch of Constantine better; but now that's tottering on its pedestal."

"Oh, that arch is all right," declared Lank;

Playing House

" I'll never go back on Constantine's Triumphal Bungalow."

" There's a well-known arch modelled after that, too," said Peter. " Where is it, my children ? "

But none of the three could answer that, so Peter said:

" Well, you are a brilliant class! Why, the Marble Arch in London, of course."

" Pooh," said Patty, " that's no more like Constantine's Arch than chalk's like cheese."

" Nevertheless it was patterned from it."

" Then they must have carried the pattern in their heads! Why, the Marble Arch is all white and smug, and sharp edges,—and Constantine's is all lovely and brown and gummy."

" Gummy ? "

" Yes; sort of fuzzy and crumbly; not as if it had just been washed up by a scrub-lady, like the Marble Arch."

" Your language is not truly technical, but I'm glad you have a feeling for arches," said Peter, laughing at Patty's scornful face.

" 'Deed I have. Let's go back and look at Constantine's Arch, while we have this one in mind."

" Come on, let's do that same," said Lank.

[121]

"And then we must be getting back to our be-
reaved parents."

"So we must," said Patty. "I forgot all
about going home. Well, good-by old sandwich man, you put up a first-class arch, I think."

"And my hotel chef put up first-class sandwiches, I think," said Peter.

"They were so," said Violet, enthusiastically.
"I don't know how you happened to think we'd
be hungry."

"Oh, when people want bread they're not
satisfied with stones, not even carved ones," said
Peter; and then they all trudged slowly up the
foot-path toward the entrance gate.

Patty kicked affectionately at the fragments of
columns and bits of carved marble that bordered
the path.

"I wonder where that used to be," she said,
pausing before a broken stone face, which
showed only the mouth and chin.

"Right under somebody's nose," said Lank,
with a grin, and Violet reproved him for being
so foolish.

"I like foolishness," said Patty, smiling at the
boy; "but I mean I wonder where the whole
statue was."

"You may as well wonder about that as anything else," said Peter. " I'm wondering if we can find a cab that will leisurely convey us home."

"By way of Constantine's Arch," reminded Patty.

They soon found a carriage and the four climbed in.

"Let's be a club," said Patty, who loved to organise things. "Then we can go and see things regularly."

"Not very regularly, the way we see them," said Peter. "But I'll join your club. Shall we call it the Roamin' Club?"

A howl of derision greeted this jest, and Lank added to the fun by saying, "No, let's just call it the Romers, and then we can Rome all around."

"Don't be idiotic," said Violet. "I propose the Wanderers' Club, that's more sensible."

"But there's been a Wanderers' Club," objected Patty; "how about the Wonderers' Club, instead?"

"Capital," said Peter. "Just the Wonderers, then we can wonder as much as we like while we're wandering."

"Flo will have to belong to it," said Patty. "She's coming to-day."

"Anybody can belong," said Peter, "who is willing to wonder."

"Shall we have regular meetings?" asked Violet.

"Oh, dear no," said Patty, "we won't have anything regular about it. We'll just meet when we feel like it, and go wondering about together."

"The fun will be," said Peter, "wondering when the next meeting will take place."

"And wondering where it will be," added Patty.

They drove home slowly, here and there catching glimpses of wonderful perspectives and splendid vistas, to which Peter Homer called their attention in his casual, humorous way.

Patty said little, but leaning back in the rather bumpy old vehicle, she revelled in the beauty all around her, and stored it away in her memory for future years.

"We've had a perfect morning," said Patty, as she joined her parents at luncheon. "Peter Homer,—we all call each other by our first names now,—is the loveliest man to go about with. He knows everything, but he never flings information at you till you want it."

"A fine trait," observed her father. "I'm like that, myself."

"Yes, you are, Daddy," said Patty, with an affectionate glance. "But even you don't know the books full of wise stuff that he does. And he's so kind and funny."

"He does seem to possess all the virtues," said Nan; "and I'm glad he's here, Patty. You seem to have several pleasant friends."

"Yes, the Van Winkles are all right. Our sort, you know. I'm glad to see some Americans once more. This afternoon Flo will come, and she's far from American, I can tell you."

A few hours later, Patty was lying down in her own room, resting after her morning's excursion, when she was roused by a tap at the door.

She jumped up and opened it, and there was the smiling face of Flo Carrington.

"You dear thing," she cried, bouncing into the room, and flinging both arms round Patty, "I'm here."

"So you are," said Patty, "and I'm awfully glad to see you. Come in, and sit down."

"I'm jolly well glad to get here," said Flo,

[125]

as she threw herself into an armchair. "The journey was horrible. Snippy almost turned back several times."

"Well, you're here now, and it's all right," said Patty, soothingly. "I'm so glad your mother let you come."

"She didn't want to; not a bit. But I teased her so, I gave her no peace till she said yes. And why shouldn't she? She's been promising me the trip for years. But she hated to have me leave her."

"She's satisfied to have you travel with Mrs. Snippy?"

"Oh, Snippy's name is really Mrs. Postle-thwaite. But that's so long, I call her Snippy for short. You must do so too, she's used to it from everybody. Yes, indeed, mumsie trusts me to her. Oh, Snippy is governess, maid, courier, chaperon, Baedeker, and book-ing office, all in one."

"And are you comfortably fixed here?"

"My word, yes! We have rooms like valen-tines. Come, see them."

Flo jumped up, and taking Patty by the arm led her to the rooms, which were furnished in the same over-ornate style as the Fairfields' apartment.

[126]

Playing House

"Snippy, dear," said Flo, "this is Patty, my very good friend."

"Pleased to meet you, miss," said Snippy, as she rose to curtsey.

She was a grim-looking old lady, one that might be characterised as a 'dragon,' but she had a gleam of humour in her eye, which went to Patty's heart at once.

"You've been to Rome before?" said Patty, by way of making conversation.

"Yes, miss, I've been almost everywhere. It's my bad luck never to be let to rest long in my own country."

"Oh, come now, Snippy," said Flo; "you're glad to be in Rome, you know you are."

"Not in this stuffy place, Miss Flo. Italian air is bad and close enough, without stifling a body with velvet hangings pulled all about. And thick carpets, snug from wall to wall. As well be shut up in a jewel-case!"

"It is exactly like a jewel-case," said Patty, laughing at the apt illustration. "All the rooms in Rome are, I believe."

"Well, I like it," said Flo; "and I'm so glad to be with you, Patty. I don't mean to bother you, you know, but you're glad I came, aren't you?"

[127]

"Of course I am," said Patty, though conscious of a feeling that Flo might sometimes be an insistent companion. But she was ashamed of this thought as soon as it came, and said, cordially; "and I'll take you to lots of lovely places. We've a new club, 'The Wonderers,' and you're to be a member of that. And to-morrow I'm giving a small afternoon tea, with you as guest of honour. It will have to be a very small tea, for I only know half a dozen people in Rome. But Floyd Austin and Caddy Oram are coming soon,—isn't that fine?"

"Yes, I like both those boys. Oh, what fun we will have. I'm so glad I came. Snippy says I have to keep up my practising every day, and study my Italian. But I don't want to,— I just want to have fun like you do."

"It's your mother's orders, Miss Flo," said Snippy, in a gruff voice of great firmness; "and her orders I must see carried out."

"You'll see me carried out if you make me work so hard," said Flo. "Tell her so, Patty."

"Can't Miss Carrington have a holiday, occasionally?" asked Patty, in her most wheedlesome way, but the stern Englishwoman shut her lips together with a snap, and then opened them to say, " No, Miss Fairfield; I have my orders."

" Wow! " thought Patty, after she had returned to her own room, " I'm glad I don't have to travel with a duenna, or whatever they call those snippy people."

CHAPTER IX

A ROMAN TEA

PATTY had decided to have her tea in the garden of the hotel, and a good-sized portion had been set aside for her use.

Light tables and chairs nestled cosily among the great palms and tropical plants, and growing flowers made masses of bloom here and there.

The orchestra, just far enough away to be pleasant, had been engaged to play at intervals, including some American airs with their other selections. The collation had been carefully chosen, and after an inspection of the place to see that everything was satisfactory, Patty went to dress for the event.

"Do you remember Smarty's party?" she said, pausing in Nan's room.

"Whose?"

"Why, there's a classic poem, something like this:

A Roman Tea

" ' Smarty
Had a party;
Nobody came
'Ceptin' Smarty ! '

And my tea will be like that! The garden looks lovely, the cakes and ices are dreams of beauty, and I mean to be a charming hostess; but, alas, my guests are so few."

"Who are coming? Every one you know in Rome, I suppose."

"Yes, but that's only Flo, and the Van Winkles, and Mr. Homer. Oh, yes, I asked Mr. Leland, but I don't know as he'll come. And Violet asked leave to bring Milly Mills, some girl she knows, whose mother is an invalid, so Milly can't go out much."

"Well, you'll have more guests than Smarty had," said Nan, consolingly. "And your father and I, and Mr. and Mrs. Valentine, will make a fine background of elderly respectability."

"Yes, you're a fine old Dowager Duchess," said Patty, smiling at pretty Nan. "With your roseleaf skin and your turn-up nose. You look more like a débutante."

"How foolish you are," said Nan, blushing

[131]

and dimpling as she always did at Patty's chaffing compliments, which were, nevertheless, sincere.

Patty was getting into her frock, a soft Liberty silk of a lovely pale green, when an impatient knock came at her door, and before she could open it, Flo flung it open and fairly rushed in.

"Patty Fairfield," she cried, "what *do* you think! That outrageous Snippy says I can't go to your tea, because I haven't done my practising! She says I can go later, but I must practise for an hour first. And I won't do it!"

"I should say not," cried Patty, in a burst of righteous indignation. "I never heard of anything so horrid. Of course you'll coax her around somehow."

"Coax Snippy! You don't know her! You see I went wondering with you all this morning, and since luncheon I've been napping, and now I want to get ready for the party."

"And you must. Come, I'll go with you and try to persuade old Snippy."

"No, that won't do any good. But here's my plan. Once in a great while, when I feel very dreadfully put out, I turn on her and scare the wits out of her. Not often, or it would lose all effect,—but I'm going to do it now. Do, if you like, come with me and see the fun."

Patty felt a little ashamed at such strenuous measures, but she followed Flo through the halls.

By the piano in Flo's sitting-room stood Snippy, a majestic figure of towering wrath and immovable determination.

"Good-afternoon, Miss Patty," she said, not uncivilly, but coldly. "Miss Flo will come to your tea a bit late, as she has her music to do."

"I'm not going to practise to-day," remarked Flo, carelessly.

"Yes, Miss Flo, you are. Not a step do you go from this room till your hour is done."

Then Flo turned to her governess and looked her straight in the eye.

"Snippy," she said, in firm, even tones, "I am not going to practise to-day, nor to-morrow, nor next day, and perhaps never again! Hush, don't you speak! I'm going to Patty's tea, now, *now, NOW!* Do you hear?" Flo's voice grew a little louder and she took a step toward Snippy, and shook a warning forefinger at her. "You have your orders, I know, but in this case you take orders from me, ME! I wish to dress at once, and you will lay out my Dresden silk with the pink bows. Now you *jump!*"

Perhaps it was the explosive way in which she pronounced the last word, but at any rate Snippy jumped as if she had been shot, and with a vanquished air went to the wardrobe for Flo's dress. Patty, overcome with amusement at the scene, slipped away, lest her presence prove embarrassing to the conquered spirit.

But she needn't have feared. Snippy's nature had a touch of arrogance and presumption because of her responsible position, and when Flo thus asserted herself, the stern old lady felt the justice of it and met the situation bravely.

"Yes, Miss Flo," she said, "and shall I do your hair with bands or a fringe?"

So the incident was closed, and never again referred to, and Flo tranquilly did her practising every day thereafter.

"Isn't she funny?" said Patty, as the two sat in the garden waiting for the guests to come.

"Yes, indeed," said Flo. "I just wanted you to see how she collapses when I go at her in earnest. But she's a dear old thing, and I put up with her domineering usually, because it's more peaceful to do so."

Then Violet and Lancaster came, bringing

A Roman Tea

Milly Mills. Patty greeted the new girl cordially, and sat down beside her for a chat.

"We're staying at a *pension*," said Milly; "mother is not well enough for the life in a hotel. I wish we might live here. You can do anything you like, can't you?"

"Why, yes, I suppose so," said Patty, smiling. "But I never think of it that way, for I always like anything I do."

Milly opened her eyes wide.

"You do?" she said. "Well, I *never* like anything I do."

"What an awful way to live!" exclaimed Patty. "Do you dislike everything on principle?"

"No, but most things are so horrid."

"Rome isn't."

"Oh, yes, it is. It's hot and dirty, and jammed full of stupid old ruins."

Milly looked so utterly disgusted that Patty felt like laughing, but controlled the inclination.

"You come with us, some day," she said. "Come with our Wonderers' Club, and we'll show you ruins that are not stupid."

"I'd love to go," said Milly, " I like you because you're so happy. I'm never happy."

"Then you're a goose," said Patty, gaily. "But I'll engage to give you a few happy hours, see if I don't."

"Well, she *is* a terror," thought Patty, as she turned away to greet some others who were coming in. "I'll have to study her out; so far, she's all fuss and fret, but she must have some good traits. How do you do, Mr. Leland. This is awfully kind of you, to come to my little tea. Won't you sit here by Miss Mills?"

It was a mischievous impulse that made Patty put the distinguished Mr. Leland to entertain fretful Milly, but to her surprise the two were soon chatting pleasantly.

"I thought she must be some good," said Patty to herself, with a feeling of satisfaction at her own insight.

"Seeing a green whisk of femininity among the bosky glades, he quickly made his way thither."

When Patty heard this speech in a high-pitched monotone, she knew at once who had come, and turning, with a glad smile, she held out both hands to Floyd Austin.

"You dear boy," she cried, "I'm so glad to see you!"

"You dear girl," he responded, "I'm so glad

A Roman Tea

you're glad. My word! but we're gay and festive, aren't we? Are you always so gorgeously social as this?"

"No, this is a special occasion to get us all acquainted, and afterward, we're to be just plain, everyday chums."

"I see; and who is the elderly youth talking to the pretty crosspatch?"

Patty fairly giggled at his quick and apt descriptions.

"Elderly youth is just the right term for Mr. Leland," she said, "but how *did* you know that pretty Milly Mills is—well, not exactly of a sunny disposition?"

"Oh, I can tell by the lines of her thumbs," said Floyd, nonsensically. "But, tell me, how does your own sunny disposition thrive in Rome? Dost like the pictures?"

"I do like the pictures," said Patty, with a little sigh, "if there weren't so many millions of 'em."

"Yes, there are some few, but then you need see only one at a time."

"But it's the same theme over and over. I get so tired of Saint Sebastian and his arrows, and Susannah, and that everlasting Thorn Extractor."

[137]

"He isn't a picture."

"No, it would be a pleasant change if he were."

"It would be a pleasant change and a wise plan, too, if they set the Thorn Extractors to picking the arrows out of Saint Sebastian."

"Indeed it would! And if they'd tie old Susannah to a tree, she wouldn't look so silly as she usually does."

"I fear your art instincts are frivolous. Come over here, Caddy, and hear Young America talk art."

Caddy Oram, who had come in with Floyd, but had paused to speak to Nan, now came to greet Patty.

"Aren't you properly awed by the art galleries?" he asked.

"I was, at first," said Patty, truthfully, "but now, I'm so used to being awed that it doesn't bother me so much."

"That's the worst of it," said Caddy, "one does get used to being awed in Italy."

"But that's the best of it," declared Patty; "if I kept on being as awed as I was the first few days, I'd be having nervous prostration now."

"I say, here comes old Homer," cried Floyd, as Peter came around a palm and joined them.

[138]

A Roman Tea

Then there was more greeting and hand-shaking and the boys clapped each other on the shoulder, and at last the young people all drifted together, and Patty thought it a good time to propose that the newcomers should join the club.

"It isn't a regular club," she explained, "because it has no regulations. We call it the Wonderers."

"I wonder why," put in Austin.

"Then you can be a member," returned Patty, promptly; "you've qualified!"

"I'll be a member too," said Caddy Oram. "I'm the best wonderer you ever saw. I can wonder at anything."

"Well, you're all members," said Patty, "and you can go on the wonder-wanders when you like and stay home when you like. Now to-morrow morning the club is going to St. Peter's, and if there's time, we may wander into the Vatican. To be sure St. Peter's is flub-dubby, but——"

"What!" interrupted Peter Homer, in amazement.

Patty dimpled roguishly.

"Yes," she went on, "as architecture, the interior is pure flubdub."

[139]

At this Homer went off in peals of laughter, and Mr. Leland, who was conversing with Mr. Fairfield, overheard, and gave an appreciative nod at Patty.

"You're right," Peter said, at last, "quite right! But how did you know it?"

"Oh," said Patty, laughing, "I'm a born architect."

"You must be!" said Peter, still smiling, "'flubdub' indeed!"

"Now to proceed with our plans," said Patty. "All who will go wondering with us to-morrow morning, open your mouth wide and say 'Ah!' which is our club motto."

Loud "ahs!" came from every throat, and the trip was decided upon.

"I'm president of the club," went on Patty, "and Mr. Homer is guide, philosopher, and friend. The rest of you can be any officers you choose. It's nicer to elect ourselves than each other."

"So it is," agreed Floyd Austin, "I'll be treasurer."

"That's an easy office," observed Patty, "as we have no dues of any sort. Mr. Homer just pays for everything, and then afterward we pay him back."

A Roman Tea

"Simple methods *are* the best," agreed Austin. "Still, I'll be treasurer, and then, if any money matters do happen, I can look after them."

"I shan't seek any office," said Cadwalader Oram. "I'll let it seek me. Probably one will hunt me up in a day or two."

"I'm sure of it," said Patty. "You're more apt to find your right niche that way."

"You talk as if I were a statue. Perhaps I'll find my niche waiting for me in the Vatican."

"Well, don't be a Thorn Extractor," said Patty, "or I won't even look you up in the catalogue. What will you be, Milly?"

"I'll be another president," said Milly, unexpectedly. "I can't bear to play second fiddle."

"Good!" said Patty. "Let's all us girls be presidents, and then the boys can be all the other officials."

So it was agreed that they should all meet next morning at nine o'clock for a visit to St. Peter's.

"Unless we start early," said Patty, "we'll never get there."

"How bright of you to see that," said Lancaster, admiringly; "and I say, everybody must bring postcards."

"I can't; I'm saving mine," said Floyd Austin.

"Saving them! What for?" asked Violet.

"To make a bed quilt," he replied gravely; "they make a lovely one. You tie them together at the corners you know, with bits of tiny ribbon."

"What a goose you are," said Patty, laughing; "you're just foolish enough for our club. Save your postcards then,—you can look over mine."

"And mine," said Flo. "I've a bigger pack even than Patty."

"I've something better than postcards," said Floyd, as he produced a small, thin, red book. "Have any of you seen this?"

None of them had, so Floyd explained.

"It's a little panorama sort of thing," he said, as he exhibited its pages, "with pictures of all the Roman places of interest. But the beautiful part of it is the description of each sight. It is evidently written by an Italian, whose linguistic lore is limited. You see on each page is an English paragraph, and also the same information in German, French and Italian. Listen, I'll read you the note about the Piazza of St. Peter's. 'This majestic place of elliptical form with the vast front of the Cathedral and the imposing Cupola, masterpiece of Michelangelo that it appears to elevate itself to the

[142]

A Roman Tea

Heaven, forms with the two round porticos in four rows of columns all what here is of more sumptuous. For enjoying the most fine panorama it must go until to the Cupola of St. Peter. By the summit of this monument the town is extending under our eyes with all its remarkable buildings. Not so far there is the Tiber. This historical river on dragging along slowly its waters, divides the city into two unequal parts. In front, by a side we see the Alban mountains, of Tivoli, of the Sabine, and by the other, the sea that with its sweetness seems that our weakened eyes are reposing for the view of so much beauties.'"

"Oh, I say, Floyd," broke in Peter Homer, "are you reading that as it is?"

"Yes, truly," said Austin. "Isn't it great! Just listen to this: 'On the right of the majestic place is elevated the Vatican that is a whole of palaces containing all what can be of more rich in the world.'"

"It's perfectly delicious," said Patty, as soon as she could for laughing. "I must have one of those books."

"I'll give each of the club members one," said Floyd. "They're cheap little affairs, the postcard men sell them; but the pictures are really

[143]

good, and you never heard anything so funny as the descriptions."

"Indeed they are funny," agreed Peter. "We'll each carry a copy wherever we go. Read us a little more." But just then tea was served, and the young people turned their attention to that interesting episode.

Floyd Austin sauntered over and took a seat beside Milly Mills.

"Delightful music, isn't it?" he said, with intent of opening a conversation, and as the orchestra was really a fine one, he expected the girl to agree.

"I hate music while I'm eating," was the surprising response, and Floyd looked at the girl to see if she were jesting.

But Milly's discontented face showed that her remark, however ill-timed and ill-tempered, was sincerely meant. "Do you, now?" said good-natured Floyd. "What a pity! You must be bothered to death here."

"Oh, I don't live here. I wish I did. I live in a most uninteresting place. Isn't Miss Fairfield lovely?"

"She certainly is," said Floyd, looking at laughing Patty, as a pleasant contrast to this pouting girl. "She's so sunny and happy."

A Roman Tea

"Yes; she must have everything she wants."

"Do you know, I think she'd be sunny if she didn't have everything she wanted."

"Well, then, it's because she happens to be of that disposition," and Milly sighed, as if that settled the matter.

As Floyd didn't consider it his place to lecture a comparative stranger on the ethics of contentment, he changed the subject and talked of lighter matters. And so infectious was his own merry disposition, that he made Milly forget her discontent and smile so gaily that she was really charming.

CHAPTER X

THE WONDERERS

IT was simply pouring sunlight when the Wonderers set off next morning.

They started early, for as they all agreed, luncheon time in Rome comes sooner than anywhere else.

They went in a large omnibus sort of affair which held them all.

Snippy accompanied them, for the simple reason that she wouldn't remain behind; but as she was a most amiable person, except when reprimanding her young charge, nobody objected to her presence.

Milly Mills was the only unwelcome member of the party. It did seem as if that girl was never in a good humour. If it looked cloudy, she feared rain; if the sun shone, it hurt her eyes. The omnibus was too jolty, too shut-in, too slow-going. Nothing pleased her and she pleased nobody. But Patty felt sorry for the girl, for she really had no one to take her about, so it was decided that she was to go with the Wonderers whenever she chose. The young men politely tried to entertain her, but she met their advances with a cold negligence, or a sharp retort, and thus discouraged their well-meant efforts.

But the irrepressible gaiety of the others could not be seriously impaired by one unhappy nature, so the fun and chatter went gaily on as the old vehicle lumbered along.

"Of course," said Lancaster, "if this chariot *should* follow the example of the One-hoss Shay, and go to pieces all at once, I suppose we could walk the rest of the way."

"The rest of the way to where?" asked his sister.

"Why, to wherever we're going. Where *are* we going, anyway?"

"We're going to St. Peter's," said Patty, firmly. "I'm president, and that's my decree."

"Presidents don't make decrees," said Flo; "you sound more like a Roman Emperor. But I'd as lieve go to St. Peter's as anywhere."

"You're a careless lot," said Peter Homer, "now I'll be the director-in-chief of this expedition, and we'll go first to the Church of the Capuchins."

Patty's Pleasure Trip

"*What* for?" said Milly Mills, so suddenly that Patty fairly jumped.

Milly had a queer little habit of saying "What for?" with a strong emphasis on the "what," and the aggressive way in which she fairly exploded the words always annoyed Patty.

But Mr. Homer answered Milly very gently, and said:

"To see some mural decorations that I'm sure you will enjoy for their oddity and strange effects."

"I hate mural paintings," said Milly, in a resigned tone, as if her wishes made little difference, as indeed was the case.

"But these aren't paintings,"

"Oh, stucco, I suppose. Well, that's worse."

"But these aren't stucco," said Peter, smiling in spite of himself at Milly's unreasonable crossness.

"No, they're stuck on," said Floyd Austin, and Peter added, "Yes, sort of appliqué work."

"What are they?" asked Patty, her interest aroused by the smile in Peter's eyes.

"Wait till you get there, and you'll see."

"If we ever *do* get there, alive," said Lank, as the stage rumbled over a bit of bad road and swayed sideways.

[148]

" Is there danger? " cried Milly, in dismay.

" There's always danger in Rome," returned Peter.

" I say," broke in Floyd, " do you remember, any of you, Rollo's very excellent rule about dangers? "

" No," said Patty. " What was it? "

" I don't remember myself. But when I was a little chap, I used to love ' Rollo in Rome,' and one of those page headings was just those words: ' Rollo's excellent rule about dangers.' Now, if we only remembered it, we could put it to use."

" I know it," said Milly, smiling for the first time that morning.

" You do! Good, the country is safe! Tell it to us."

" Why, you know, that funny Mr. George was going about with Rollo, and he told him not to go too near the edge of some place. So Rollo said, ' You may go as near as you think safe, Mr. George, and I will keep back an inch from where you go.' ' Very well,' said Mr. George."

" Right you are! " said Floyd, " that it! But I suppose it doesn't apply to this case exactly. However it's splendid to remember if we're in the right sort of danger at any time. Don't you just love Rollo, anyway?"

"Yes, indeed," said Milly, brightening, "and Mr. George too; he was so indulgent. He always said 'Very well,' no matter what Rollo wanted to do."

"I'm not like that," declared Peter Homer. "I expect you all to say 'Very well,' to whatever I want to do. So first we'll go in here to the Capuchin Church. Alight, everybody."

Their lumbering vehicle stopped, and they all went into the old church.

Its unadorned and unattractive exterior made Patty wonder why they came there, and the interior was not much more interesting.

Mr. Homer made his little band of wonderers pause while a monk drew aside a curtain and revealed Guido Reni's famous painting of "St. Michael and the Enemy."

They all enjoyed the short description Mr. Homer gave them of this picture, and then they went on through the small side chapels and downstairs to see the decorated walls of which Peter had spoken.

When Patty saw what the decorations were composed of, she could scarcely believe her eyes. Room after room they went through,

[150]

and on each wall and ceiling were elaborate and intricate patterns, worked out in human bones.

The party was conducted by a Capuchin monk, who walked ahead and pointed out the curious details.

The monk wore a long brown robe with a cowl, and a rope about his waist.

Patty thought he looked sad, and she said so to Mr. Homer.

"Monks always look sad," he replied, "it's part of their costume."

As the monk could speak no English, he told them about the bones in Italian, and Peter Homer translated for the benefit of the others.

"He says," said Peter, "that all these decorations you see on walls and ceilings are the bones of four thousand monks, who have in the past belonged to this monastery. The designs are called mosaics, but, properly, they are appliquéd patterns."

The Wonderers gazed in real wonder at the strange effects. Just such designs as would be used to adorn a painted or gilded salon were here carried out in bones. Long arm or leg bones, radiating from a centre, formed a conventional star; rosettes were made of rings of

[151]

overlapping shoulder-blades; and delicate traceries were woven of ribs and smaller bones.

Or there would be a frieze of skulls, interspersed with geometrical figures made with hundreds of finger joints, and collar-bones.

Here and there, in a niche, was a complete skeleton, in a, mouldering robe so old that it scarce hung together. Sometimes these skeleton monks reclined in a recess lined with skulls and bones.

It was all most curious, and though somewhat gruesome, Patty was fascinated at the strange sight.

"Ask him if he likes it," she said to Peter, and when asked, he answered at great length, and very earnestly.

"What does he say?" asked Patty, impatiently.

"He declares," said Peter, "that to be used in this decorative way is the greatest honour a Capuchin monk can have. To gain it, a monk must have been in the monastery for twenty-five years, and he's awfully afraid he'll die before he earns his right to be a fresco."

"Ugh!" said Milly, with a shiver, "I hate it! Let's go out into the sunlight."

So Milly and Violet, with one or two of the

others, went on out of the crypts, but Patty lingered to see a little more of the strange cemetery.

"I suppose the whole gentlemen are more honoured than the dissected ones," she said.

"Yes," said Floyd, "and they seem all broken up about it!"

"Don't jest," said Patty. "I think it's very impressive and interesting. Oh, look at that lamp!"

A hanging lamp swung from the ceiling, and the bowl of it was made of skulls surrounded by vertebræ, while the chain-like suspension was made of many femurs, fastened end to end.

"I simply must have postcards of these," said Flo, and they asked the grave monk if they might buy them.

Apparently he had never heard of postcards, for Peter could not make him understand. At last he offered them photographs, and they all bought some. Afterward they did find some postcards, but it was at an outside shop, and the monk, who never went outside his restricted limits, knew nothing of them.

"That's the most wonderful thing I've seen yet!" said Patty, as they returned to their lumbering old carryall.

"I think it's terrible," said Milly; "don't let's talk about it!"

So out of deference to their somewhat difficult member, they dropped the subject, but Patty never forgot the Capuchin monks who approve of such a strange way of venerating their dead.

To St. Peter's they went next. Mr. Homer hustled them all out of the stage before they entered the Piazza, saying they must fasten a picture of it in their memory.

"You can't see the best view of the church if you're close to it," he said. "Stand here," and he paused before they entered the great colonnaded circle.

And there he made them stand, for fully five minutes, without speaking, while they photographed the scene on their mind.

"Isn't he great?" whispered Patty to Flo, as they were released, and allowed to go forward.

"Yes, indeed. I never saw anyone who knows so well how to make sight-seeing instructive, without being a bore."

"Inside the church," said Peter, as they were about to enter, "you may wander and wonder as you please. I've no word to say, for it's too big to talk about as a whole, and we haven't time now to discuss its parts. So look about you as you like, and crane your necks up at the dome, or admire the frantic allegories on the walls, as you prefer."

" I want to see St. Peter's statue," said Patty, "but I don't want to kiss his toe."

" Here it is," said Homer, leading her to the great bronze statue. As they looked at it, many visitors approached, and kissed the bronze toe, which, owing to the height of the pedestal is just about at the level of a person's head.

Invariably the devotee wiped off the toe with his handkerchief, before setting his lips to the sacred shrine, and Patty was amazed to find, on a closer inspection, that the great bronze toe was nearly all worn away.

" But it isn't worn by the kisses," said Patty; " it's worn by the handkerchiefs!"

" That's true," said Peter; " and it's a good plan to use a handkerchief, but I think it's a better plan to omit the osculation entirely."

" So do I," agreed Patty, " but what a lot of people have dabbed at it to wear away that solid bronze!"

" They have indeed. Now I'll show you some of the other statues."

They paused before several of the best sculptures, and Mr. Homer told their history in a short, simple way. Patty enjoyed it all, and even Milly seemed to be interested. The others staid to listen, or drifted away and came wandering back, as the fancy took them.

Perhaps Snippy appreciated Mr. Homer's talk more than any of the others, for she was well versed in artistic lore, but she remained quietly in the background, and let the young people chatter by themselves. As they left the church, they found it had turned cloudy, and the sky showed decided appearance of almost immediate rain.

" Just the thing! " cried Mr. Homer. " I've been waiting for a good shower. Jump into the 'bus."

They scrambled in, thinking they were about to return to the hotel, but Peter told the driver to go to the Pantheon.

" Why, it's going to rain," said Patty.

" I know it; that's why we're going to the Pantheon. Its roof leaks."

" What *are* you talking about? "

" Just what I say. Have you been to the Pantheon? "

" No, not yet. Why? "

" Well, as you perhaps know, it's open at the

The Wonderers

top. There's a hole twenty-six feet across, and as the Pantheon has no umbrella, it rains in."

Milly was laughing to herself at this conversation.

"What are you giggling at?" said Patty, a bit surprised to see Milly amused.

"Why," said Milly, "that's exactly what Rollo did. As soon as it began to rain he flew to the Pantheon to see it rain in!"

"I didn't know that," said Peter, smiling. "I fear I am sadly deficient in my 'Rollo,' but it is really a good plan to fly to the Pantheon when it rains, for it's not always easy to get such an opportunity."

After they reached the Pantheon, and were inside, Patty understood why it was a desirable thing to do.

It was a sudden and very hard shower, and the strange effect of the rain coming in at the open skylight was curious indeed.

The only opening in the Pantheon, save the entrance door, is the large round hole at the top of its domed roof. This is open to the sky, and sunlight and rain alike come in.

Many people stood round the edges of the circular church, but the centre of the floor was wet with the driving rain. So swift were the

[157]

drops that they spattered up again as they struck the stone floor, and it was like hundreds of tiny fountains. But save for the wet circle on the floor, the place was dry and pleasant. They looked at the various tombs and monuments, and then inscribed their names in the book which is there for that purpose.

"It's wonderful," said Patty, gazing reverently around the great room as they were leaving, "but I should think they would have a canopy of some sort over that hole in the ceiling."

"They did," said Peter, "but the shutter, or whatever it was, is lost, and has never been replaced."

"Why not, I wonder," said Patty.

"I wonder," said Peter.

It was their good fortune that the shower was but a short one, and when they reached the street again the rain had stopped, and soon after the sun shone once more.

"I'm glad we had that opportunity," said Patty; "for it almost never rains in Rome, and I shall always remember that circular shower."

"Now," said Flo, "mayn't we go to a shop before we go home?"

"*What* for?" said Milly.

"Trinkets," replied Flo. "I'm making a memory chain."

"A what?" said Patty, eagerly, for it sounded attractive.

"Why, you get a chain," explained Flo, "a slender silver one, you know; ana then you get all sorts of little jigs to hang on it."

"Jigs?"

"Yes; little carved ivory elephants and monkeys; little silver things of all sorts, or bronze or wood, or anything. Come on into a shop and I'll show you. Mr. Homer, you must know the right kind of shop, don't you?"

"I think so," he said; "but, Miss Mills, where did Rollo go, for this purpose?"

"I don't think he made a 'memory chain,'" said Milly, pleased to be consulted; "but the description of his shopping for a Roman sash is very funny."

Patty secretly wondered if Milly had ever read any other book beside "Rollo," but she realised that she didn't yet know the girl, and indeed she wasn't easy to get acquainted with.

Peter took them to a fascinating little shop, where there were all sorts of tiny wares, at prices not exorbitant; and the girls all bought trinkets for memory chains.

"Don't get too many at once," said Flo to Patty. "You know you must buy some in Florence or Venice, or wherever you go. Get something appropriate to the city,—if you can."

Patty bought a little silver cat, for she said she remembered seeing cats all over the Forum and Coliseum; and especially in Trajan's Forum. Then she bought a tiny column, and a little model of the Arch of Constantine, and several others.

The men didn't seem to want memory chains, but they each bought a tiny trinket to carry as a pocket-piece, as a memento of the Wonderers' Club.

CHAPTER XI

ROMAN PUNCH

IT was a very rainy day, so the excursion which the Wonderers had planned had to be postponed.

And so they were gathered in the Fairfields' pleasant sitting-room, trying to make believe they didn't care to go out.

In this attempt they all succeeded better than Milly, who was distinctly and aggressively cross.

"Milly," said Peter Homer, in his kind way, after one of her petulant outbursts, "it's raining, and I'm glad it is, and you're going to be glad too. You're going to have such a good time this afternoon, that you'll go home saying you're glad it rained so we couldn't go driving out the Appian Way."

"I won't do any such thing," declared Milly. "How could I like it better to sit cooped up in a stuffy old parlour than to go for a lovely drive?"

"Wait and see, my child," said Peter. "Now, my Wonder friends, I'll tell you my plan. Let's start a paper, a nice little paper, and we'll all contribute."

"And publish it every week?" cried Patty, who loved to write things.

"Yes, for one consecutive week, anyway. I'll be editor-in-chief, and you can all be department editors, and choose any department you like. If I were to suggest, I'd say let Patty Fairfield be the fashion editor, for she always wears such masterpieces of sartorial architecture."

They all laughed at Peter's description of Patty's pretty frocks, and she said:

"Well, I'm glad you didn't call my clothes flubdubby, anyhow. Yes, I'll write your fashion column. What will you write, Milly?"

"I don't know yet, but I'll write something. Shall we do it now?"

The girl's face had brightened wonderfully. Peter had discovered that she had secret leanings toward literature, and he felt sure that his plan for the afternoon's amusement would appeal to her.

"Yes, we'll begin at once," he said. "If Patty can provide paper and pencils. You may

[162]

each have a half hour, and then must turn in your copy, finished or not."

Patty found plenty of stationery, and went about, distributing it to her guests.

"I can't write a thing," declared Flo, "but I'll draw a picture. Is it to be an illustrated paper?"

"It will be," said Peter, "if illustrations are contributed."

"I'll do a Limerick," said Caddy Oram. "I just love to do Limericks."

"Let's having missing line ones," said Violet.

"All right, you do that kind then. Everybody can do just what he or she likes."

"We must have the paper uniform," said Patty, "so we can bind it all together afterward."

"Yes," said Lank Van Winkle, "then we'll have typewritten copies made for each of us."

"If we want them!" put in Floyd. "I'm not sure this crowd can write a volume worthy of undying fame."

"Traitor! put him out!" cried Lank. "If he's so weak-hearted, I'll write his contribution."

"Weak-headed, you mean," said Peter. "No,

everyone must write his own. Now, what shall we choose as a title for our paper?"

"Is it to be a humourous publication?" asked Floyd.

"Yes, indeed."

"Then listen, lend me your ears, and prepare to receive my suggestion with thunders of applause, for I am about to offer you the best, and indeed, the only title for the journal."

"Huh," said Lank, "if it's the only one, you deserve little credit for thinking of it."

"Wait till you hear it," said Floyd, undismayed. "If you don't applaud, I'll know you don't appreciate true cleverness. I propose, ladies and gentlemen, that we call our weekly paper, the *Roman Punch.*"

He was indeed greeted with applause, and every one agreed that his suggestion was the very thing.

"Then you see," he went on, "we can model it after the London *Punch,* only it will be funnier."

Then they all set to work, and as no pretensions to real literary excellence were expected, they rapidly scribbled a lot of nonsense.

Floyd finished first, and began bothering the others.

Roman Punch

"I'll help you, Patty," he said, sitting down beside her.

"No, don't speak to me. The depth of my subject requires concentration of thought. You go away."

So Floyd wandered over to Flo's side, and criticised her drawing.

"Ho! ho! if I couldn't draw better than that! Here, let me take your pencil."

But Flo only gave him a terrible frown, and he backed away, cowering in pretended terror.

But at last the half hour was up, and Peter announced that the manuscripts must be handed in, whether finished or not.

"What luck!" cried Caddy Oram, who had been working diligently, "I've just four lines of my Limerick done, so we can make a 'missing line contest' of it."

"Let's call in father and Nan to hear the reading," said Patty, "and Flo, why don't you invite Snippy, if she'd like to come?"

"Oh, she'll adore to come," said Flo, and ran in search of her governess.

So the audience was increased by three, and then all sat in readiness to hear the paper read.

Peter and Floyd had arranged the pages, and

[163]

had added a sort of introduction, and by unani-
mous invitation Peter was induced to read it.

So in his pleasant, deep voice he read:

"The *Roman Punch*. A journal written by
members of the Wonderers' Club during their
Roam in Rome.

"There may be further numbers and there
may not. Subscription limited.

"The first selection is an exquisite poem by
our popular poet, Mr. Floyd Austin. You will
notice the marvellous dexterity of his rhyming,
as well as the delicate beauty of his imagination.
It is called:

"'A RHYME OF A ROMAN

"'An old Roman, known to no man,
    Without friend and without foeman,
    Without title or cognomen,
        Is the subject of my pome.
    And the Roman, never homin',
    Still is roamin', still is roamin',
    In the dawn or in the gloamin',
        See him roam and roam and roam
        All about the streets of Rome.'"

This effusion received great applause, until the
modest poet hid his face in his hands, quite overcome at the ovation.

[166]

Roman Punch

"There's something so tragic about it that it makes me weep," said Nan, wiping her eyes with her handkerchief.

"It's the noble numbers that affect you, my dear," said her husband. "Grandeur of thought is always impressive."

Floyd's contribution made a great hit, and then Peter went on to read another.

"The next is a fine Limerick by Miss Violet Van Winkle. It throws light on a hitherto mysterious subject, and it justifies what has often been considered a cruel deed of a bloodthirsty emperor. I refer to the late Mr. Nero, and his burning of his native town. The true facts of the case are here set forth:

" ' " Well, yes," said Tiberius Nero,
    " I frankly admit I'm a hero.
        But it wasn't for ire
        That I set Rome afire,—
    The weather was quite down to zero." ' "

There was a moment of silence, and then Floyd said, slowly, "Oh, I see! He kindled the fire to warm himself!"

"Yes," said Violet. "It was a cold winter that year."

" 'Twas a chilly day for Nero, when the mercury went to zero," said Caddy; "but I say, was Nero's name Tiberius too?"

" No," said Violet, unabashed, " but it needed that to fill up the line nicely. And anyway, it may have been. Those old Romans had lots of names besides the ones they used every day."

" Of course they did," said Patty. " And I'm sure he was Tiberius Nero,—it sounds so natural that way."

" Next we come to a picture," went on Peter. " This gem of art is the work of our talented wonderer, Miss Flo Carrington. I will hold it up that you may see it, but as its merit can only be appreciated by a closer inspection, we will pass it around the circle. It represents Miss Fairfield hugging her very dear friend, the Coliseum."

Flo's picture was really clever. Though only a slight sketch, it showed a very good caricatured likeness of Patty. Her arms, abnormally long, were embracing the Coliseum, which, with a happy smile, was enjoying the occasion.

Patty declared she should keep the picture and have it framed, and Mr. Homer said she might do so, after he had photographic prints made of it for them all.

[168]

Roman Punch

"The next," continued Peter, "is a poem by our talented member, Miss Milly Mills. This is a most creditable composition, and quite appropriate to our paper. I think, to do it full justice, it should be read by its author. Miss Mills, won't you read your verses yourself?"

Flattered by Peter's kind words, Milly took the paper and read her own lines aloud. It was a really good, humorous jingle, and as Milly read it, each of the others felt surprise that she could do such clever work.

"A ROMAN COIN

"There once was a queer Roman boy
(Though equally queer he would deem us!)
    A nice child was he,
    Born 40 B.C.
And named Regulus Romulus Remus.

"His queer and ridiculous garb
    Was Roman from toga to sandal;
    He ate for his lunch
    Some cold Roman punch,
By the light of a large Roman candle,

[169]

" One day he had finished his meal,
    And went for a walk in the Forum;
        He made counter-marches
        Beneath the big arches,
    With banners and flags floating o'er em.

" When he found, lying right in his path,
    A Roman coin called a denarius;
        Dated 40 B.C.
        He exclaimed, ' Goodness me !
    That's the year I was born ! How hilarious !

" ' I'm sure it will bring me good luck,
    This coin, with its date, B.C. 40.'
        And so he went roamin'
        About in the gloamin',
    With his Roman nose held high and haughty.

" But stay ! There's a flaw in this tale,—
    A coin of that date is peculiar !
        I don't think you'll see 'em
        In any museum,
    I just told about it to fool yer !

    "Why, Milly," cried Patty in delight, " I
think that's fine ! I'd no idea you were such
a poet."

Roman Punch

"That isn't poetry," said Milly; "it's just jingle."

"And mighty good jingle," said Nan. "But why was the coin peculiar? Didn't they have coins in 40 B.C.?"

"Oh, Nan," said Mr. Fairfield, "stop and think! How could a coin be *dated* 40 B.C.?"

"I don't see why not. Doesn't that mean forty years Before Christ?"

"Yes, but B.C. is only used since A.D. began."

"Oh, of course! I see. They didn't use B.C. until the time meant by B.C. had gone by!"

"Exactly that," said Mr. Fairfield. "But, Milly, that's a first-class little jingle, and I think you're in a fair way to become a verse-maker."

Milly blushed with pleasure at the compliment, and her face lost entirely its usual discontented expression.

"So that's her ambition," thought Patty to herself. "I'll have a good talk with her about it when I get a chance. Perhaps I can help her."

It was the delight of Patty's life to help any-body, and she felt sure she could aid Milly, if only by sympathetic interest in her literary products.

[171]

"Now," went on Peter, "we'll listen to some very wise wisdom from the pen of our young American philosopher, Mr. Lancaster Van Winkle. He has chosen to favour us with a collection of proverbs. I will read them, for I know his natural modesty will make him too embarrassed to listen to the sound of his own voice. The first gem of priceless wit is this:

"'Rome is where the Art is.'"

At this punning, a general groan was heard from the audience.

"Cheer up," said Peter, "worse is yet to come."

"'A Roman stone gathers no moss.'"

"I don't see any sense to that," remarked Flo.

"There isn't any," said Lank, amiably, "but it somehow sounded as if there ought to be."

"It *does* sound so," said Patty, encouragingly; "go on, Peter."

"'The Coliseum is the thief of time.'"

"That's a good one! What next?"

"'Where ignorance is bliss, 'tis folly to study guidebooks. One touch of Baedeker makes the whole world kin. Tourists will happen in the best regulated ruins. He who Romes and roams away, may live to Rome another day.'"

Roman Punch

"I think they're great!" said Floyd. "I want a copy of those."

"Thank you!" said Lank, with a bow to his admirer.

"Now," said Peter, "we come to a column of fashion notes, by our esteemed friend, Miss Fairfield, who is an authority on the subject. I will read it to you.

"'Fall fashions for Rome. This season cabmen will continue to wear the tattered and disreputable costumes which they have (apparently) worn for the last decade.

"'Tourists will wear short skirts, and a look of inquiry. Roman citizens have discarded togas and tunics, and now wear any old thing. Their appearance is not so picturesque as formerly.

"'Americans and Britishers visiting in Rome will wear Roman sashes a great deal this fall, as they think it gives them a touch of local colour. They will also wear memory chains.

"'Visitors who have already been to Naples, are wearing pink coral necklaces.

"'There is little change in the fashions for statues. As a rule these people seem not to care much for clothing, and what they wear is scanty of material and shows little, if any, trim-

[173]

ming. The statues are not wearing hats this year, and their styles of hair-dressing, though picturesque, are a bit untidy.' "

"Good for you, Patty!" cried her father. "That's good fooling, my child. You may turn out a blue-stocking yet."

"I don't think so," said Patty, doubtfully; "I had pretty hard work to grind that out. I'm glad you like it."

"It's very waggish," said Snippy, in such a matter-of-fact tone that the others had to laugh.

"Now that's real praise, Mrs. Snippy," said Peter Homer.

As Flo's governess objected to her own name, and preferred the funny title Flo had given her long ago, the other young people compromised by prefixing a Mrs., which seemed, at least, a little more respectful. They had all grown to like the strong-willed and dictatorial old lady, and her approval of the fun of the *Roman Punch* pleased them.

"Now," said Peter, "we come to the last contribution. It is the work of the distinguished Englishman, Cadwalader Oram, better known as Caddy. Indeed, he's so fond of afternoon tea, I might call him Tea-Caddy.

Roman Punch

Well, as he hadn't quite finished his immortal Limerick verse when the bell rang, we'll call it a missing-line contest, and we'll all have a try at it. Have you a prize, Patty, that can be given to the successful one?"

"That's the beauty of Rome," said Patty. "You do nothing but collect articles that are just right for prizes. I'll have enough to last me all the winter for card-parties and such things at home. Here, I'll give you this little model of the Temple of Saturn, in Parian marble."

"Pooh, we've all got those already," said Violet, "and anyway, they break if you look at them."

"You must give softer glances, then," said Austin. "But, Patty, something a little less ubiquitous would suit me better too."

"Well, here's a little silver statuette of St. Peter," said Patty. "How's that?"

"A whole lot better! I'll try hard to win that."

"But I don't understand the contest part," said Patty; "what do we do?"

"Why, Caddy has written four lines of a Limerick," explained Peter. "I'll read those,— you may jot them down if you like. Then,

[175]

each tries to write a fifth line, and whichever is judged the best gets the prize."

"Who's the judge?"

"Well, I'll appoint Mrs. Fairfield and Mrs. Snippy to judge the efforts. Now, listen; here are the first four lines:

"'There was a young tourist from home,
    Who Baedekered all over Rome.
        Said a lady, "My dear,
        Do you like the things here?"

Now, you see you must each make a fifth line."

"Oh, that's easy," said Milly, who was a born rhymer.

They all sat silently for a few moments, scribbling, or nibbling, at their pencils.

"It's harder than I thought," confessed Patty. "I can't think of a thing that rhymes and makes sense both."

At last the lines were done, and given over to the judges.

"We've decided," said Nan, soon after. "But we'll read first the ones that did not win the prize. They're all awfully good, I think. Here's Patty's first; shall I read the four lines?"

[176]

Roman Punch

"No, we all know those; just read the fifth."

"Very well, this is it. 'She said, *not* when they say "write a pome!"'"

"That's capital. Are the others better?"

"Some are," said Nan, going on. "Here's Floyd Austin's; 'She said, "Well,—I have bought a pearl comb."'"

"Oh, I think that's good," cried Patty, "I'd give that the prize. Go on, Nan, this is fun."

"This is Flo's. '"Well,"' she said, '"it surpasses Cape Nome."'"

"That's all right! Next!"

"Here's Lancaster's: 'She said, "All except St. Peter's Dome!"'"

"Whew! I suppose she tried to climb it," said Caddy. "I did once!"

"This is a good one," said Nan; "it's Violet's; it *almost* took the prize: 'She said, "No, I like our Hippodrome!"'"

"Oh, that's fine!" cried Patty, clapping her hands. "Why didn't I think of that? It was so hard to find a rhyme."

"But here's the prize one. It's Milly's. I think you'll have to yield her the palm for composition. I'll read the whole this time.

[177]

" ' There was a young tourist from home,
Who Baedekered all over Rome.
  Said a lady, " My dear,
  Do you like the things here? "
She looked up and answered, " Why, no'm." '

You see, this fits into the spirit of the first part so well. You can fairly see the young tourist bored to death, tired, hurried, flurried, dazed, with sight-seeing, but bound to go on with it; why should she like things here? Oh, Milly, yours is best."

Most of them agreed with this, and though Flo and the two Van Winkles secretly thought Milly's line rather commonplace, they didn't say so.

Then the pretty prize was bestowed on Milly, and her eyes shone with pleasure and justifiable pride in her own success.

And when the party broke up she said to Mr. Homer:

" I've had a lovely time, and I'm *glad* it rained, and we couldn't go driving."

" That's a good girl," he responded, " and I'm jolly glad you took the prize, and we'll have that drive yet, too."

CHAPTER XII

PATTY AND PETER

IT was the day before the Fairfields were to leave Rome.

Patty and Peter Homer sat on one of the upper flights of the Spanish Steps, waiting for Flo and Snippy, who were in a neighbouring shop.

The beginning of the sunset hour cast a warm, happy light, and Patty, who was very sensitive to the peculiar charms of this most delightful part of Rome, was gazing at the beautiful staircase that seemed to ripple down from the Church of Trinita dei Monti to the fountain below.

Peter had called her attention before to the construction of these steps, and she had learned to love the wonderful effect as they separated and joined again, like a cascading river.

"Why is it that steps are so beautiful?" she said to Peter, who was also enjoying the view.

"Not exactly because they are steps," he re-

[179]

plied. "A flight of stairs is not necessarily beautiful. But when designed by a master mind, with knowledge of architectural effect and symmetry, they can be made to express a great deal. But don't try too hard to understand, just look at it all, and wonder."

"I do. And I shall always remember this, my last afternoon in Rome, sitting here in the sunset——"

"With me," interrupted Peter.

"Yes, with you. I have to thank you for much of my pleasure in Rome. Without what you have told me and taught me, I should not have known anything about the real Rominess of Rome."

"You don't know much about it yet, nor do I. But we've seen a little of it together, and I, too, shall always remember our good times here."

"Very frivolous times. What a lot of fun we've had with our foolish picnics and games."

"Yes; but you know Italy of itself is not a humorous country. Whatever fun one gets out of it, one must take to it."

"I wonder you're so fond of fun," said Patty, musingly, "when you're so sentimental."

"What! I? Sentimental? Never! I'm the most practical man in the world."

"Oh, yes, you're practical enough, but you're sentimental, too."

"And aren't you?"

"I don't know. No, I don't think I am."

"I don't think you are, exactly, either. But I think you will be some day. And as a beginning, couldn't you cultivate a little sentiment toward me?"

Patty looked around her,—at the gold and violet sunset sky above them, the sparkling fountain plashing below them, the soft twilight atmosphere about them, and the Roman monuments both near and far,—and answered:

"If I ever could be sentimental, it would be here and now."

"Nonsense!" cried Peter. "I don't want you to be sentimental! Save that for Venice. Child, don't you know the difference between sentiment and sentimentality?"

"No," said Patty, in surprise, "is there any?"

"You're hopeless! Doesn't this exquisite moment, here and now, inspire you with impulses of noble sentiment quite removed from mawkish sentimentality?"

"I don't know," said honest Patty. "What sentiment ought I to feel?"

"Oh, I don't want to suggest. Look in your

own heart, and tell me if there's no pleasant thought there, for this especial moment,—and for me?"

Patty shut her eyes tight, and pondered.

"Yes," she said, triumphantly, "I know what you mean. I looked in my heart, and it's overflowing with a sentiment of gratitude for your kindness to me."

For once Patty saw Peter Homer look positively angry.

"You ought to be ashamed of yourself," he exclaimed; "or, rather, I ought to. I should know better than to expect a child like you to have any real feelings."

"I'm not a child!" said Patty, offended in her turn. "I'm over eighteen, and I've lots of real feeling, but as you don't seem to care for it, I won't waste it on you!"

Peter laughed at the indignant look on Patty's pretty face, and said, gaily: "You've plenty of time, little one. Your sentiments are sprouting, and they'll grow rapidly enough, once they're started. Thank Heaven, your sense of humour will keep them from growing too rank. Now, soothe my wounded feelings by telling me you've a nice kind sentiment of friendship sprouting in your heart for me."

"Sprouting! Why, my friendship for you sprouted long ago. Now, it's grown to a big tree, and on every leaf is written a kindly thought of you."

"Ah, you *have* imagination; and that's closely akin to sentiment. Dear little Patty, I wish I could teach you to see life as I've taught you to see Rome."

Patty looked up quickly, surprised at the note of earnestness in his voice, and found Peter's dark eyes looking steadily into her own.

"I wish you could," she said, simply, as her own clear blue eyes frankly returned his gaze.

"Being desirous of making the acquaintance of the pretty girl on the steps, the wayfarer sat down beside her," declaimed the ridiculous voice of Floyd Austin, as he appeared before them, and dropped down on the step beside Patty.

"Why, Floyd," she cried, "I didn't see you coming. Where have you been?"

"Seeing Rome, and hoping I'd see you, which, by good luck I did. What are you two babes in the wood doing here all alone?"

"Waiting for Flo and Snippy. They're in that shop over there, buying photographs."

"Um,—yes. Don't you care for photographs?"

"I've bought all I can carry, already. I shall have to use them for wall paper, when I get home. It would take a Maine forest to frame them all."

"I saw a room papered with photographs once," said Peter. "They were divided by narrow mouldings, you know, but the pictures were pasted right on the walls."

"Wasn't it horrid?" asked Patty.

"Awful. Photographs in great quantities are awful, anyhow. But, while we're on the subject, won't you give me one of yourself? To hang on my memory chain, you know."

"I'd ask for one too," put in Floyd, "but I've seven of you already, Patty. Snapshots, but good ones."

"I don't see why he should have seven, and I none," said Peter, in a plaintive voice.

"I'll give you one," said Floyd, generously.

"No, thank you,—I don't want it. But what I do want, Patty, is to take a snapshot of you, right now, here on the Spanish Steps."

"You've no camera," said Patty.

"I can get one in a minute, in that photograph shop. They keep all sorts, and I'll just borrow one long enough to take you. May I? "

"Yes, if the light's good enough. I don't care," said Patty, indifferently.

Peter looked at her curiously, and then went off for the camera.

"Having achieved his heart's desire, the young man tripped gaily away," said Floyd, mischievously smiling at Patty.

"Here comes Flo," cried Patty, as Snippy and her charge appeared, laden with long pasteboard rolls. "Now we can all be in the picture."

"So we can!" said Floyd. "Homer will be *so* pleased!"

Mr. Homer returned with his camera to find a group ready posed for him.

Floyd had arranged them, and Snippy sat on one step, with her arms outspread in a classic attitude, while the two girls stood demurely with clasped hands on either side, a step below. Floyd, above and behind, held out one hand with beneficent gesture, and in the other was a long pasteboard roll, which he used as a trumpet.

"It's an allegorical group," he announced, of ' Fame blessing a bunch of Tourists.' "

[185]

Entering into the spirit of the thing, Peter focussed his camera, and secured what afterward turned out to be a delightfully ludicrous picture.

"Now," said Peter, in the tone he used when he had no intention of being contradicted, "I will take a picture of Patty alone.

"All right," said Flo, not caring, and she turned away to talk to Floyd Austin.

"Lean lightly against the balustrade," said Peter, as Patty stood carelessly on the steps. She fell into the position he had suggested, and against the background of innumerable steps, above, below, and on either side, the girlish figure stood out in fair relief. The white serge frock, with its graceful long coat opening over a soft white blouse, was a becoming style to Patty, and suited well the scheme of the picture. Her soft, white, felt hat, turned back from her ripply, gold hair, and a filmy white Liberty scarf trailed from it, and fluttered over her shoulder. She was the embodiment of quiet, graceful, American girlhood, and the picturesque Roman surroundings accented her charm.

Peter Homer held his breath as he adjusted the camera.

"Don't move," he begged; "it's perfect."

"I've no intention of moving," said Patty, calmly; "take your time."

It was one of the girl's best traits that she was never self-conscious; and so she was never embarrassed at posing for a picture. In fact, she rather enjoyed it, as she was fond of photographs of all sorts.

"All over," announced Peter Homer, as he snapped the camera for the last time. "Now, if you people will wait till I take this machine back to its home, I'll invite you all to tea right here and now."

"Goody!" cried Patty; "I'm starving, and they have the loveliest cakes in this tearoom of all Rome."

Snippy was graciously pleased to accept the invitation, and soon they were gathered round a tea table, and Patty had all the cakes she desired.

"When can we see the pictures?" asked Flo.

"As soon as I can get them developed. You may each have copies of that stunning classic group you posed in, but the landscape of Miss Fairfield is all for my little own self."

"Can't I have one?" asked Patty.

"No, madame. They are not for general circulation."

" Pooh! " said Patty, " I don't want a picture of myself, anyway. I'd rather have one of you."

" I'll send you one," said Peter, quietly.

" Not being members of the picture exchange, the other guests turned their attention to tea and muffins," said Floyd, in a resigned way, as he appropriated more muffins, and begged Snippy to pour him another cup of tea.

" It doesn't seem possible," said Flo, " that we've been here over a month; does it, Patty? "

" No, indeed, seems more like a week. Oh, I know I shan't like Florence as well as Rome, and then, too, all you boys won't be there. I do love boys," said Patty, contemplatively, as she broke a bit of frosting off her cake and gazed at the two young men before her.

" Thank you, old lady," said Floyd. " And do you class this stalwart gentleman and my-self among your beloved ' boys '? "

" Oh, I don't know. I suppose you *are* too old to be called boys; but anyway, you're the ones I meant. You and Lank and Caddy. Why, I'm so used to having you all bothering around, I'll be awfully lonesome in Florence, I know I shall."

" You'll have me," said Flo. " I'm nice."

" Yes, you are. And perhaps we'll have more

fun without the boys. 'They do tease so,' as *Alice* said about the elephants."

Patty's roguish smile contradicted her speech, and both men knew it.

"Don't be so sure you won't see us in Florence," said Floyd. "My ticket is most accommodating; isn't yours, Homer?"

"No," said Peter, shortly. "At least it doesn't include Florence among its coupons."

"I'm sorry," said Patty, gently. "I'd be glad to see you there. Are you really coming, Floyd?"

"I don't know yet. How long shall you be there?"

"About a fortnight, I think. Perhaps longer. It depends on how father and Nan like it."

"And you?"

"Yes, and I. But I'm so good-natured I always agree with them."

"That's a good one!" said Floyd, "when it's well known that you're the dictator of the Fairfield Forum."

"Only when I care," said Patty, "and I don't often care."

"Well, I care that you're going away," said Floyd, "and I shall follow you, if possible, as soon as I can."

CHAPTER XIII

A NOBLE SOLDIER

THE Fairfields were to leave Rome for Florence at ten o'clock in the morning, and Flo and Snippy were to go with them. Patty's regret at leaving Rome was somewhat lessened by her father's promise that they should return there for a week or two after visiting Florence and Venice.

"For you know, Father," she said, "I really ought to come back here and brush up my memories of Roman history, before going back home."

"Yes," agreed Mr. Fairfield, "particularly as your knowledge of Roman history is confined to picnics in the Forum, lunches on the Palatine, and tearooms on the Spanish Steps."

"Well, I do know a few important facts about the Roman Emperors; and if I get them mixed up, that's because there were so many of the Emperors and so few of me."

"You're a frivolous puss, Pattykins, but as

you're on a pleasure trip, I don't suppose you can take time for useful information."

" But that's just what I do get. Dusty, musty, fusty knowledge about the inner workings of the Roman Empire isn't a bit useful to a great, big girl like me. And the varied bits of information that I pick up with both hands as I go along will cheer and amuse me all my life."

" I believe you're right, you wise child. You know how to have a good time, anyway, and I'm glad of it. Now, run along, and say your good-bys to that flock of young people waiting for you."

Patty was all ready to start on their journey, and her travelling costume of blue Rajah silk that just matched her eyes was both appropriate and becoming. Her straw hat was trimmed with blue roses, which, though not of Nature's tint, were most harmonious, and she wore a long filmy blue veil, which was a characteristic article of her attire.

" Why do you always have these uncertain things trailing around you, Patty? " asked Floyd, as an end of the veil brushed against his cheek.

" Oh, they're so comforting," laughed Patty,

as she disentangled her scarf from his grasping fingers.

The Wonderers had gathered in the palm garden to say good-by to Patty.

Milly Mills was in tears, for Patty had been very kind to her, and the strange, silent girl had learned to love her dearly.

"I wonder what we'll do without our Patsy," said Violet, as she caressed Patty's hand.

"Follow her up," said Lank, promptly. "I've been trying to persuade the governor to go on to Florence, and though he says no, he's sort of half-hearted about it. Perhaps you can coax him 'round, sister."

"Perhaps I can," said Violet, smiling hopefully. "I'll try anyway. And if not, we'll meet in New York, won't we, Patty?"

"Yes, indeed. We're going to have a reunion there some day, and all the Wonderers will walk on Broadway and Fifth Avenue, hunting for something to wonder at."

"And finding it, too!" said Lank. "We'll show Europeans that little old U. S. A. is O. K."

"Sounds like a riddle," said Caddy Oram. "But I'm going to the States some day, and indeed we will have a reunion. If we can't have the whole eight at once, we'll reune, a few at a time."

"Do come," said Patty, cordially; "all of you, whenever you can."

Then they all exchanged addresses, and promised to write letters, and send pictures, and meet whenever possible, and then the hotel omnibus was at the door to take the travellers to the station.

"Come, Patty," said her father, as she lingered for a last word to Milly, "you'll make us all miss the train if you spin out your farewells any longer. Hop in, now."

He helped Patty into the omnibus, jumped in himself, and then they were off, leaving the young people and Mr. and Mrs. Van Winkle waving handkerchiefs after them.

"Isn't it funny?" said Flo, after they were settled in their chairs in the train, and rolling toward Florence, "how, as soon as you leave one place, your mind flies ahead to the place you're going to?"

"Yes, it is," agreed Patty. "Now, I just love Rome, and I love that whole bunch of people we've left behind us, but I'm already wondering what Florence will be like. What's it like, Snippy?"

"Well, Miss Patty, it isn't a bit like Rome, to begin with."

"No; I suppose not. There are no ruins."

"No, miss; but there are beautiful gardens, and pictures and statues till you 'most wear your poor eyes out."

"Yes, and break the back of your neck. Picture galleries are worse than quinsy sore throat."

"But that's in front," said Flo, laughing. "Pictures make you ache in the back of your neck."

"They make me ache all round," declared Patty. "I love 'em, but they wear me out."

"Oh, Patty," cried Flo, "look at the orchards with the trees tied together! Isn't it lovely?" Patty looked from the window at the thick ropes of grapevines which festooned one tree to another in the orchards past which their train was flying.

"Great!" she exclaimed, her eyes shining at the beautiful sight. "They look like the Alpine travellers, who are roped together for safety."

"Nonsense," said practical Flo, "what's the use of roping yourselves together if you're standing still? They're not moving."

"Well," said Patty, "our train goes so fast that it makes them look as if they were moving; so it's well they're tied together."

"You're a goose," remarked Flo, as if that settled the matter. "I say, Patty, isn't this a funny car?"

"I suppose it is to you," said Patty, looking around at the drawing-room car they were in.

"It's unusual in Italy, I'm sure, and I never saw one like it in England; but it's exactly like the parlour-cars we have in America."

"Is it? Well, I like it a lot better, like this, where we're all in one room, and can see our fellow passengers, than to be shut up in those little compartments and only see our own party."

"Yes," said Patty, doubtfully; "but the other way is more cosy. I've no desire to see my fellow travellers, have you?"

"Yes; I like to look at them, and wonder what they're like. For instance, see those two young Italian men, over there. I'm sure they're nobles, counts probably. Aren't they handsome?"

"Flo Carrington, you stop looking at handsome young Italians or I'll call Snippy's attention to you."

"Oh, they don't know I'm looking at them."

"Don't they, indeed! Well, they do, and you must stop it."

"I have stopped," said Flo, looking out of the window. "But aren't they stunning?"

They were handsome young fellows, and had an air of dignity such as might well befit an Italian noble. Flo and Patty demurely refrained from glancing at them, save for a furtive glance now and then, but Flo declared she must make a sketch of them. She undertook it, but the train jolted too much to make drawing a pleasure, so she abandoned the project. Soon the guard came through, asking for those who wished to lunch in the dining-car, and tickets were given for seats at table.

"I perfectly love to eat on an Italian train, don't you?" said Patty, as they found their places for luncheon.

"Yes, I do," said Flo, "except I don't like the spaghetti and things they love to eat."

"Oh, I do. And I'm sure when I get home I can cook macaroni in true Italian fashion, and delight all my friends."

"It wouldn't delight me, I hate it. But I love the fruit." And well she might, for the rich luscious fruits of Italy are surpassed nowhere on the globe, and they are bestowed on travellers in unstinted quantities.

Mr. and Mrs. Fairfield sat at one of the tables arranged for two, while Snippy and the two girls sat at a quartette table.

As there was thus a vacant seat, another passenger was assigned to it, and to the surprise and secret glee of the girls it was one of the young Italian men they had noticed in the other car.

Flo and Patty looked down at their plates in an effort not to smile at each other, and Snippy glared at the young man as if he were an intruder.

Presently he made a civil remark in Italian, and as Snippy was able to talk fluently in that tongue, she answered him, politely, but rather shortly.

" Doesn't he speak English at all? " said Patty, with great interest.

" No," said Snippy, sternly, " eat your luncheon and don't look at him."

" Good gracious! " said Patty, secure in the knowledge that the stranger couldn't understand her, " I don't want to look at him. But I just want to know if he's a count. Do ask him,

[197]

Snippy dear. Flo thinks he is—and I think he isn't."

" Well, he isn't, Miss Patty. He's a soldier."

" A soldier! How interesting. Can't we talk to him a little, Snippy, with you to translate, you know."

Snippy hesitated. The young man was exceedingly polite and well-bred, and had already asked if the young ladies spoke Italian. Even her careful instincts could suggest no reason why they should not converse, with herself as interpreter.

So, in very conventional language she introduced Signor Grimaldi to her two young charges, and he bowed with the ease and grace of a distinguished cavalier.

" Ask him where he's going," said Patty, who knew that Snippy would frame the question less curtly.

A few words of Italian passed between them, and then Snippy informed the waiting ears that the Signor was going to Florence.

" What hotel? " asked Flo, and the information was soon gained that he was going to the same hotel that they were themselves.

" Heavenly! " said Patty, rolling her eyes, dramatically. " Tell him we're enchanted, and that we think he's a lovely man, and that he looks as if he had just stepped out of a comic opera, and that——"

"There, there, Miss Patty, how you do run on. I shall tell him none of those things. He's a very chivalrous gentleman, and I don't want him to think you a forward young person."

"He can't think anything about me, Snippy, except what you tell him. So tell him I'm a lovely lady,—a duchess, disguised as an American."

"He'd never take you for a duchess, Patty," said Flo; "tell him I'm a duchess, Snip, and that this other young woman is my maid."

"I'll tell him nothing; I'm ashamed of your foolishness, Miss Flo." And Snippy proceeded to eat her luncheon with such a dragon-like air that the Italian soldier wondered what he had done to deserve reproof.

Presently he spoke again to Snippy, regarding the scenery, and to make amends for her previous coolness she answered him affably. Then there ensued an interested conversation, for Snippy was a cultivated and well-informed woman, and the young man was courteous and entertaining.

Besides which, he was greatly attracted by the

two pretty girls and wished the duenna would bring them into the conversation.

"The young ladies,—have they visited Florence before?" he asked finally, in Italian, and Snippy felt in honour bound to pass the question on in English to eager Patty and Flo.

"We must answer prettily," said Patty, with a demure face, though her eyes were dancing, "or else Snippy won't let us talk to him at all. Say to the Signor, please, that we have never before been in Florence, and does he think we'll like it."

Snippy sniffed a little, but translated the message to the Italian.

"The Signor says," she translated again, "that he is sure you will like Florence and Florence will like you."

"Remark to him," went on Patty, "that we thank him for his politeness, and we'd like to know if the gentleman who was with him in the other car is travelling with him, and what is his noble name."

"The other gentleman is with him. His name is Signor Balotti, and he too is a soldier."

"Then," put in Flo, "inquire of his soldiership why they are not fighting."

"He says," resumed Snippy, "that they do

[200]

not fight because there is no convenient war. But he does not regret that, since it gives him opportunity to meet three charming ladies."

"Oh, Snippy-Snip," said Patty, "are you sure you're translating truly? Didn't he say one charming lady, and two ill-mannered girls."

"If he didn't, it's only because he is himself too polite to say so," said Snippy, but there was a twinkle in her eye, and Patty could see that she had quite decided in favour of the young man's desirability as an acquaintance.

They all rose from the tables then, and Snippy introduced the Italian to Mr. Fairfield. Though not fluent in the language, Mr. Fairfield could make himself understood, and while the ladies returned to the drawing-room car, he remained behind for a smoke and a chat with the young man.

When he returned, he electrified the two girls and Nan by telling them that Signor Grimaldi was a very desirable acquaintance indeed, as was also his chum, Signor Balotti. The men had arranged to meet them again in Florence, and would doubtless be a decided acquisition to their circle.

"I told you so!" said Patty. "I knew he was the salt of the earth as soon as I looked at him."

" Pooh, I told you so first," said Flo. " But I wish he could talk English. I don't care much about knowing people I can't talk to."

" Nor I," said Patty. " I hope we will find some Americans or English at the hotel."

They reached Florence about mid-afternoon, and drove directly to their hotel, on the bank of the Arno.

" What a lovely river ! " said Patty. " At least it's clean. The Tiber is so yellow, and so is the Thames. The Seine isn't much better,—indeed none of them can compare with our own Hudson."

" But this whole place is beautiful," said Flo, as they looked from their cab on the trees and gardens of beautiful Florence.

The day was very warm, and there was a glare of sun everywhere, so our travellers were glad to reach their hotel and go right to the apartments awaiting them.

Flo and Patty had communicating rooms, and had soon exchanged their travelling costumes for teagowns and were waiting for the tea which they had ordered sent up.

They peeped out between the slats of their blinds, and saw the river directly below them.

" Isn't it picturesque ? " said Patty. " I love

it already. After an hour or so, father says it will be cool and pleasant for a drive, so we'll see a little of the place this afternoon."

" Lovely," said Flo, " but here's our tea, Patty, so come and drink it."

CHAPTER XIV

CARLO AS GUIDE

THE first night that Patty spent in Florence she awoke about midnight, thinking she heard music.

"I must have been dreaming," she said to herself, and then, again, she heard lovely strains, as of some one singing outside her window.

She jumped up and ran to peep through the blinds. Sure enough a small crowd of people stood in the white roadway that divided the hotel from the river, and four men were singing beautiful music. The others were passers-by, who had stopped to listen, and who stood about or sat on the low parapet.

"I'm being serenaded!" thought Patty; "it must be by those two Italian soldiers!"

Flinging on a kimono, she flew into the next room to wake Flo.

"Get up!" she cried, shaking the sleeping girl. "Get up! Signor Vaselino, or whatever his name is, is serenading us!"

"What?" murmured sleepy Flo.

"Oh, get up, you slow thing! Get up first, and understand afterward. Here's your dressing-gown,—here are your slippers. Put your foot in!"

Jamming the worsted slippers on Flo's bare feet, Patty gave her one more shake and succeeded in fully wakening her.

They went to Flo's window, and opening the blinds, stepped out on the little balcony.

It was a perfect night. Although the first of October, it was warm and balmy, and the great full moon cast a golden glow on the smooth water of the Arno.

The four men who were singing wore picturesque Italian costumes, and their broad-brimmed hats, turned up with feathers, gave the effect of a comic opera chorus.

The bright moonlight made the shadows of the people clear and distinct along the white road, and the river, with the buildings rising on its other bank, was a perfect background.

"Isn't it great!" whispered Patty, squeezing Flo's arm. "Do you suppose it's our Italian friend that we met on the train?"

"No, you goose," said Flo, laughing. "This isn't a serenade especially for us. They're professional singers, and they're serenading the whole hotel. See the other people on their balconies."

Sure enough every room in the hotel that had its own balcony showed its occupants standing out there to enjoy the music. And windows that had no balconies were thrown wide open, and faces appeared at each.

"Well," said Patty, "this is a nice country, where the opera singers give free concerts at midnight."

"They're not entirely free," said Flo, who seemed to know more about the matter than Paty. "Observe what now happens."

The song came to an end, and after flourishing bows, the quartette stood expectantly waiting. Soon something was thrown from a window, and, as it fell in the road, one of the singers stooped for it, and then they all bowed again.

It was a coin flung by one of the hotel guests, and it was quickly followed by others, until the singers were all four scrambling on the ground picking up the coppers and small silver bits that had rained down upon them. Sometimes a coin was flung wide of the mark, and this was picked up by the idle bystanders and usually given to one of the singers.

Then they sang again, and this time Patty ran for her purse, to take part in the recognition of the music. After this song, she and Flo threw down coins too, and it was great fun to watch the musicians pick them up. Probably from much practice they were very deft at this, and as the hotel was a large one and well filled with people, they reaped a fine harvest. At last, having doubtless noticed American voices among their audience, they sang Yankee Doodle, though a very much Italianised version of that classic composition. However, it struck a patriotic chord, and from many of the hotel windows American voices joined in the chorus. After this tribute to her native land, Patty flung down all her small change, and finally the minstrels wandered away to serenade some other hostelry.

"Wasn't that fun?" said Patty, as she and Flo returned to their rooms. "I think Italians must be very honest people, or the others would have taken the money instead of the singers."

"Perhaps they did," said Flo, "or some of those others may have been friends of the singers who picked up the money for them."

"Well it's a pretty trick," said Patty, "much nicer than hand-organs, I think."

"Yes, or street pianos," agreed Flo; "and now if you'll kindly go back where you belong, I'll return to my own slumbers, and don't wake me up again to-night, if the United States Marine Band comes over to give a concert."

"Indeed I won't, you ungrateful creature; I'll just enjoy it all by myself."

So Patty went back to bed and slept until the sun shone high over the Arno, in place of the moon.

The weeks in Florence passed rapidly, it seemed to the two girls. Each day Patty grew to love the beautiful city more.

"It goes along so smoothly," she said to Nan, one day. "In Rome we were always flying around after some excitement, but Florence days just flow by, all exactly alike."

"Why, Patty, I think our days are varied a great deal," replied Nan, who was tying her veil, and was devoting most of her attention to that.

"No, they're not. We always go to picture galleries in the morning. And shopping or for a drive in the gardens in the afternoon, and then dinner takes up most of the evening. But I like it; I'm not complaining at all. And I'm learning heaps about pictures. I didn't know

I could learn so much just by looking at them. Why, some of my favourites, I almost feel as if I had painted myself."

" It must be fine to have such a good opinion of yourself," laughed Nan. " Where are you going this morning? "

" Oh, Snippy's laid aside with a headache, and as you and dad are going off on an excursion, he said Flo and I might go out with Carlo."

" Well, have a good time. We'll be back by tea time, so be in the palm room by five. Some people are coming."

Nan ran away to go off on a day's jaunt with her husband, and Flo and Patty put on their hats to go for a drive with Carlo.

This very useful Italian citizen was a well-trained guide, who had been recommended to Mr. Fairfield by an old friend. Carlo was experienced in all styles of sight-seeing, and moreover was trusty and reliable in every way. So Mr. Fairfield allowed Flo and Patty to go with him to galleries and museums, and Carlo proved a most satisfactory cicerone and chaperon. To-day the cab came to the door and Carlo assisted the two girls into it.

" Where to, ladies? " he asked, as he stood at attention.

"Oh, I don't know," said Patty; "we've seen 'most everything. Where shall we go, Flo?"

"To Dante's House," was the prompt reply. "We haven't seen that."

"All right," said Patty; "to Dante's House, Carlo."

"Non, ladies, non," was the unexpected reply. "To the great galleries? yes. To the great monuments? yes. To the gardens? yes. But to a house—a so plain, uncertain house—which in maybe Dante was born,—maybe no,—no, we do not go to Dante's house. It is a foolishness."

Patty laughed. She well knew Carlo's dictatorial ways, and if he didn't think Dante's House worth seeing, it probably wasn't.

"I don't care, Carlo," she said, "go where you like. It's a lovely morning, and I'm so amiable I'd follow anybody's advice. You don't care; do you, Flo?"

"Not a bit. Let's leave it to Carlo."

"Then, ladies, I take you once again to the Baptistery. I wish you to look again at the bronze doors of Ghiberti."

"Go ahead," said Patty. "I know those doors by heart; I know what Michael Angelo said about them, and I have both sepia and

[210]

coloured postcards of them. But go on, we can't have too much of the bronze doors."

Carlo, though he spoke English, was not always quick enough to grasp the whole of Patty's raillery, but he saw she was willing to follow his advice, so he took the seat beside the cabdriver, and they rumbled away.

When they reached the Baptistery, they stood in front of the great doors, and listened patiently while Carlo repeated the meanings of the designs. It was owing to these repeated descriptions of Carlo's that Patty was acquiring a really good appreciation of painting and sculpture, and though she mildly chaffed the good-natured guide, she listened thoughtfully to his lectures.

"You're a fine guide, Carlo," she said; "you told all that exactly as you told it last time. I think you're the best guide in all Florence."

"Oh, no, lady," said Carlo, with a gesture of deprecation. "Verra pore guide. I simply do my best to serve the kind patrons who honour me. I speak but only eight of the languages."

"Only eight?" exclaimed Patty, in a teasing tone, for she well knew this was mock modesty, and Carlo was really proud of his linguistic acquirements.

"Yes; eight. It is but few."

"Oh, well, it will do for us," said Patty; "I only know one, myself."

"That is enough for a lady," said Carlo, so gallantly that Flo and Patty laughed.

"You know a lot of languages, Carlo," Patty said, "and better than that, you can be tactful in all of them."

"Ah, I am a Florentine," said Carlo, bowing, with native pride in his birth that he scorned to admit in his acquirements. "But, ladies, here comes a so good opportunity. A bambino--a baby—is arriving for baptism. We will go in and observe the ceremony."

"We will, indeed," said Patty. "I've always just missed it, before. Come on, Flo."

Inside the Baptistery they went and found a priest and a few officials gathered around the font.

With great interest they watched the baptism of the tiny three-days' old infant. The little one was carried by its father, and accompanied by a nurse and an Italian lady, presumably an aunt or other relative. The child was robed in a grand conglomeration of laces, ribbons, jewelry, and swathed in voluminous outer wrappings.

After the short ceremonial was over, the girls lingered to look at the mosaics in the choir, a study in which Patty was taking a great interest.

As they stood there Patty heard a voice over her shoulder, addressing her in Italian. She turned, and saw the Italian soldier, Signor Grimaldi, accompanied by his friend Balotti.

They had not seen these men since the meeting on the train, and they had wondered what had become of them.

"Oh, Signor, how do you do?" cried Patty, quite forgetting that he couldn't understand her.

But he understood the smile and gesture and shook hands cordially with Patty and Flo, and then presented Signor Balotti.

This introduction was in Italian but the girls assumed its intent, and smiled pleasantly at both men, though at a loss how to continue the conversation.

"We can talk through Carlo," said Patty, with a sudden inspiration. "What's the use of his eight languages if he can't help us out in a case like this? Carlo, these are two friends of ours, but they can't speak English, nor we Italian, so you must act as interpreter. See?"

"Yes, lady," said Carlo, a little hesitatingly. "They are your before acquaintances?"

[213]

"Oh, yes," said Patty, laughing at his air of caution; "we met them on the train coming from Rome. At least we met Mr. Grimaldi, and were properly introduced. Ask him why he hasn't been to see us."

Reassured, Carlo talked to the young men, and translated back and forth for the benefit of both sides. It seemed that the Italians had mistaken the name of the hotel where the Fairfields were, and had not been able to find them, they themselves being at a different one.

"But I spik a very small Angleesh," volunteered Signor Balotti, timidly, and the girls turned to him in delight.

"Oh, do you?" said Flo. "Then you can help us all out."

So they chatted away, and as each only understood about a quarter of what the other said, the conversation was mostly laughter and gestures.

At last with the help of Carlo the young men conveyed to the girls an invitation to visit some certain of the Royal apartments in the Pitti Palace, which are not usually shown to visitors.

The idea appealed to Carlo, who wanted his patrons to see all that they could, but he hesitated about accepting the escort of these handsome young strangers.

"Oh, yes, we'll go," cried Patty, after she learned of the invitation; "don't be a goose, Carlo, you're worse than Snippy! I'll take the responsibility, and I'll tell father all about it, and he'll say, 'Bless you, my children.' Come on, Flo."

Then turning to Signor Bolotti, she smiled, and said:

"Si, signor, we will go avec pleasure."

The polyglot sentence was not very intelligible, but the smile was, and Carlo allowed himself to be persuaded to carry out the plan.

Their cab was dismissed, and a larger carriage called, which would hold the four, and again Carlo climbed to the seat beside the driver, and they were off.

Conversation was now difficult, but that made it only more interesting.

"Where do you live?" asked Patty, choosing a simple question as a beginning.

This Signor Balotti understood, but his reply was entirely unintelligible, and as Patty didn't care where they lived, she gave it up.

"The Boboli gardens are very beautiful," volunteered Flo, willing to do her share to break a silence that might become embarrassing.

"Boboli? No—not this hora," said Balotti, with a regretful smile.

"Goodness!" said Flo, "he thinks I'm asking him to take us there, and he says not at this hora. That's hour, isn't it, Patty?"

"Yes. She doesn't mean we want to go there, but that it is beautiful,—bella,—bellissimo! See?"

"Si," responded Balotti, repeating, without understanding.

"So pretty, you know," Patty floundered on; "so green and trees, and flowers,—flora,—gracious, Flo, what is Italian for flowers, you ought to know!"

"I don't," said Flo; "but, look this way!" and Flo sniffed vigorously at an imaginary bouquet. Her dramatic instinct was so strong that her meaning was quite evident, and one could almost imagine she had beautiful flowers in her hands.

"Si, si, si!" exclaimed the gallant Balotti, and with an order in Italian for the driver to stop, he sprang from the carriage and flew over to a neighbouring flower stand. He returned with two huge nosegays which he bestowed upon the girls, with a voluble flow of Italian compliments.

Carlo as Guide

"Oh, Patty," said Flo, blushing with mortification, "he thinks we asked him for flowers!"

"Si, si, *flowers!*" said Balotti, beaming with pleasure at having gratified the wishes of the young ladies.

To Patty's surprise Carlo took the flower episode calmly, and she concluded that a gift of flowers in Italy must mean even less than in America.

"Yes," said Carlo, when she asked him this; "yes, the Signori mean to present the compliments they cannot speak, by means of the so beautiful bouquets."

"Thank them very much," said Patty, "they are most kind."

But her own smiling bows of appreciation were quite as welcome to the gallant Balotti as Carlo's expressed thanks.

And now gloom settled on the handsome face of Signor Grimaldi.

"He wants that he too," said Balotti.

This seemed obscure, at first, but the discontented expression helped Patty's quick wit, and she exclaimed, "Oh, Mr. Grimaldi wants to give us flowers also?"

"Yes," said Balotti, "or—or another."

"Yes," said Flo, assisting him, "or something

else. Well, Patty, we must accept another gift, —I see that clearly. What do you suggest that we can take with propriety, and thus bring smiles to Grimaldi's face as well as Spaghetti's, I mean Balotti's?"

Patty looked about on either side.

"Postcards!" she exclaimed, as she saw a vendor with his tray.

"Just the thing!" cried Flo. "Tell 'him, Carlo, that the young ladies would be overjoyed to receive the gift of half a dozen postcards each."

Carlo translated this, and Signor Grimaldi's face broke into wide smiles as he sprang in his turn from the carriage.

"Tell him only a half dozen, Carlo," warned Patty, for Grimaldi's enthusiasm betokened his buying the whole tray, and sending the man for more.

But he obeyed Carlo's strict orders, and returned, bringing Flo and Patty each six of the most celebrated monuments of Florence.

The girls made charming protestations of gratitude and appreciation of this courtesy, and the drive continued. The two Italians, pleased with their own performances, seemed content to sit and beam pleasantly for the remainder of the way, and soon they were at the portals of the Pitti Palace.

As the young men had promised they were able to show them through some magnificent Royal apartments, rarely shown to strangers, and where even Carlo himself had never been before.

The sights were most interesting, and after a pleasant hour spent there, they all drove back to the hotel. The Italian gentlemen took leave, and through the interpretations of Carlo, Patty asked them to return late in the afternoon and take tea with them, and this the young men readily promised to do.

CHAPTER XV

GOOD-BY TO FLORENCE

MR. FAIRFIELD was not at all displeased to learn that the two girls had gone to the Royal Palace with the Italian men, for he trusted to Carlo's notions of propriety, and was quite willing to abide by his decisions. But Snippy was less agreeable about it, and declared that hereafter she should go with Miss Flo wherever she went, headache or no headache.

"Now don't be stuffy, Snip," said Flo, in reply. " In the first place I don't care tuppence for those two native gallants, for I can't talk to them, and when I do, they misunderstand me."

But the two young Italians seemed much at- tracted by the whole Fairfield party, and nearly every day after that they dropped in to tea, or invited them to go on little excursions, or brought small gifts to Nan and the girls.

By degrees, too, Patty and Flo picked up a

[220]

few Italian phrases, and after a time were able to make some slight attempts at conversation, which greatly delighted the two men.

So really they added not a little to the pleasures of the Fairfields' stay in Florence, and when the time came for them to leave the Italian gentlemen were quite inconsolable.

As a parting favour they begged that the whole Fairfield party would lunch with them on their last day in Florence. This invitation was accepted, and a delightful excursion was arranged to the Cascine. Mr. Fairfield stipulated for an early luncheon, as their train left for Venice at four, and he did not wish to be hurried at the last moment.

"I hate to take an afternoon train, anyway," he said to Nan. "I like to start in the morning, and reach our destination in the afternoon. But leaving Florence at four, we won't reach Venice until ten or after."

"Well, it doesn't really matter," said Nan, "and the girls are so anxious to go to this fête of Signor Grimaldi's."

The proprietor of the hotel also reassured Mr. Fairfield.

"You are going to the Royal Danieli Hotel, in Venice," he said, "and have your rooms engaged. Well, they will meet you on your arrival, not only with gondolas, but with motorboats and steam launches, and I assure you, you will have not the least care or responsibility. Also, the whole place will be as bright as day."

So it was arranged, and the day before the party Flo and Patty packed their trunks and had everything in readiness. Also, on the day before the party, Nan received a telegram from a friend of hers, who was passing through Venice, and who urged her to come on that day, in order that they might meet.

Nan was greatly disappointed not to see her friend, but she positively refused to let them all leave a day earlier, and thus deprive Flo and Patty of their anticipated pleasure.

Patty insisted that they should do this, but Nan wouldn't agree, and at last Patty said:

"Well, I've an idea. You and father go on to Venice to-day, by the noon train. Then we'll stay here for the party to-morrow, and Snippy can take us to Venice quite well afterward."

This sounded plausible, but Mr. Fairfield said: "Here's a better plan still. Let Snippy and Nan go to Venice to-day, thus travelling by daylight, and I'll stay here with you two girls, and take you to Venice after your luncheon

[222]

party to-morrow. If any of us are to travel after dark in an unknown country, I prefer to look after the trip."

This was more sensible, as Snippy and Nan could easily catch the noon train that day, and so give Nan an opportunity to see her friend.

Hotel arrangements were made by telegraph, and Mr. Fairfield put the two ladies on the train, knowing his wife had a safe and pleasant escort in the grim but capable Englishwoman.

"We ought to do something extra gay to-night, Daddy," said Patty, "to console you for Nan's absence. It was awfully good of her to arrange it all this way, rather than disappoint Flo and me."

"Yes, I think it was," agreed Mr. Fairfield, "and I shall expect you to entertain me hilariously."

"I think," said Patty, "the most fun would be just to go for a drive, and shop somewhere and eat ices off those funny little tables that stand out on the sidewalk."

"That is indeed a daring proposition," said her father, smiling, "but I'll take you. Get your hats and wraps."

Flo and Patty were soon ready, and away they went for a drive round Florence by night.

"It isn't as brilliant as Broadway," said Patty, looking about at the fairly-well lighted streets.

"It's lighter than London at night, though," said Flo.

"Yes, or London by day, either," said Patty, who knew Flo never resented good-natured chaff.

Then to Patty's delight they stopped at a sidewalk café, and ate ices and little cakes, while they enjoyed the novel scenes all about.

Often whole families would be gathered round the tables, and little children would sit contentedly nibbling at buns or pastry.

"It's lovely," said Patty, with a little sigh, as she finished her ice; "I wouldn't live here for anything, but I do enjoy seeing it all."

"So do I," said Flo. "But I'm 'most sure I'll like Venice better than Florence. Shan't you, Patty?"

"Yes, I expect so. I like Rome better, too; but still, Florence is a lovely city. You ought to love it best, Flo, as it's named after you."

"Oh, it's pretty enough, but I've always been just crazy to see Venice."

The girls chatted away, and Mr. Fairfield smoked a cigar, and then said they must go back to the hotel and to bed, as they had a busy day ahead of them, with their party first, and the journey to Venice after.

"And I thank you, gracious ladies," he added, "for giving me a most pleasant evening."

"Glad you enjoyed it," said Patty; "I've had lots of fun, watching the people and noticing their funny ways."

On the way home they stopped at one or two shops that were still open, and bought a few more of the delightful bits of bric-à-brac in which Florence abounds.

"I'm simply overburdened now, with little boxes, and carved things, and mosaics, and plaster casts, but I must have this head of Dante."

"I've seven heads of Dante already, so I won't get one," said Flo.

"He must have been a hydra-headed monster," said Patty; "I think it fairly rains heads of Dante in Florence. But I've so many people at home who'll be glad to have one, that we're sending a lot."

The next day was fair and beautiful for their little excursion. Their two Italian hosts came for them in an imposing equipage, and they drove out to the park, or Cascine, as it is called.

Patty had been here before, but she always enjoyed the lovely place, and was glad to pay it a farewell visit. The conversation was rather limited, but they were used to that now, and laughs and gestures often made up what they could not express in words.

Mr. Fairfield liked the two young men, and endeavoured to make himself entertaining, so far as his slight knowledge of Italian would allow.

The festival ended rather abruptly, as the travellers must run no risk of losing their train, and the girls had to change their pretty, light dresses for travelling garb.

"Why are you carrying your furnished hand-bag?" said Flo to Patty, as they left the hotel. "We won't be on the train over night."

"No; but there isn't room in my trunk for it, and, too, it's convenient to have brushes and things. We don't reach Venice till after ten o'clock, and I propose to take a nap in the evening hours. I'm awfully tired now."

"So am I. Those natives tired me out."

"Well, we've seen the last of them now."

"I don't know. They talk of going to Venice."

"Oh, I hope not. Mr. Homer and Floyd

[226]

Austin are to meet us there, and I don't want those smiling popinjays bothering around."

" No, I don't, either."

The train was a comfortable one, and the party were soon comfortably settled in it.

Mr. Fairfield had not been able to secure an entire compartment for themselves, and as they occupied but three seats, an elderly Italian couple came in with them.

This left one vacant seat, into which the girls piled their wraps and some magazines and also some candy and flowers, which their gallant admirers had sent them as a parting souvenir.

They had previously asked the Italian dame, by smiles and signs, if she cared to use this vacant seat, but as she kept on her queer little bonnet, and cape, she signed that she had no use for it. Mr. Fairfield put all their bags and hats in the upper racks and they settled down for a long, but not unpleasant ride.

For a time the girls chatted, and then Patty looked over some magazines and papers, while Flo crocheted lace, which was a favourite occupation of hers. The elderly Italian gentleman was immersed in a newspaper, and his amiable-looking wife nodded as she alternately dozed and wakened.

"I think," said Mr. Fairfield, as he at last folded up his own paper, "I think I can leave you two girls for half an hour while I go to the smoking car. That kind-faced, motherly lady will do for chaperon, even if you can't talk much to each other."

"Of course," said Patty, "go ahead. There's nothing to chaperon us about, but I just adore that old lady's looks. She has the air of mothering the whole world."

"That's true," said Mr. Fairfield, looking at the lady, whose eyes were closed for the moment. "She's one of the best types of Italian matron. Well, then I'll run away for a bit. The guard has punched our tickets, so you won't be bothered, and if any luggage official speaks to you, refer him to me. They can always understand English."

He went away, and Patty hoped her father would find some one in the smoker with whom he could talk, and so while away the time.

The Italian lady looked up as Mr. Fairfield left the compartment, and at his smiling gestures of adieu, and his nod toward the girls, she quite understood that she was to lend them her chaperonage, and nodded assent with a beaming face.

Good-By to Florence

"Amerika," she said, smiling kindly at Patty.
"Si, signora," said Patty, in her pretty, polite way. "Amerique?" she asked, pointing to Flo.

"Non, non," said the dame; "Engleesh signorina."

"Si," agreed Patty, and there the conversation stopped, much to Patty's regret, for she wanted to talk to her new-found friend.

"I shall study Italian before I come again," she said to Flo; "it isn't necessary for travelling purposes,—I mean guards and hotel clerks,—but it is if you want to converse with your fellow travellers."

"Yes," agreed Flo; "but it's awfully hard to learn."

In about an hour Mr. Fairfield returned, and then they all went to the dining-car for dinner. The Italian couple went too, but they did not sit at a table near the Fairfields.

"She's lovely," announced Patty. "I call her Signora Orsini, because I feel sure she descended from that noble family."

"In that case, it would be her husband who was of noble descent," suggested her father.

"Oh, yes, so it would. Well, it makes no difference. They're Orsinis. He's as nice as

[229]

she is, only he seems a very quiet man. They scarcely talk at all."

After dinner they returned to the compartment in the other car, and found the Orsinis, as Patty called them, already there. The place had been lighted up, and presented the appearance of a cosy little sitting-room.

"These trains are most pleasantly arranged," said Mr. Fairfield. "And now I'll leave you again for a short time, and have an after-dinner smoke, then I'll come back, and before we know it, the evening will fly by, and we'll be in Venice."

"Stay as long as you like," said Patty. "I feel as if I had lived with Madame Orsini all my life, and I have a feeling she's fond of me."

"That's the beauty of her not being able to understand you," teased Mr. Fairfield, with a twinkle in his eye.

"Oh, go along! If she *could* talk to me, and understand me, she'd love me so she'd want to adopt me."

"She can't have you!" cried Mr. Fairfield, in mock alarm. "Don't come to so much of an understanding as that!"

"No, I won't. I'm not ready to leave you

yet. Now, go, Daddy, and have a calm, pleasant smoke with yourself."

" Madame Orsini " bowed and smiled, and wagged her head protectingly at the girls, as Mr. Fairfield went away.

" Now," said Patty, " I just must see where we are at. I have a fine railroad map of Italy, and I'm going to investigate it."

She spread the map out before her and she and Flo traced their route.

" You see," said Patty, " here's Florence; we left that and followed this mark to Pistoja; I remember we passed through there while we were at dinner. It's too dark now to see the names of the places, but Bologna is the next stop, and from there we go straight along this line to Venice. Oh, here we are at Bologna."

The train stopped and waited quite a time in the station. Patty and Flo were greatly interested in looking from their windows at the bustling crowd on the platform. It was brightly lighted, and travellers were hurrying about, jostled now and then by vendors with trays or push-carts.

" Stop that boy," cried Patty, " let's buy some grapes."

They called the boy, who came to the train window and sold them great bunches of delicious grapes, which Patty laid aside for an evening repast.

"Why do they stay here so long?" asked Flo.

"I don't know," replied Patty, "unless they are taking on a load of sausages. Isn't this the place where they make Bologna sausages?"

"No, you goose, of course it isn't."

"Oh, I think it is," and Patty turned questioningly to the Italian lady.

"Bologna? Sausages?" she said, with an inquiring smile.

"Bologna, si," returned the dame, but "sausages" she could not understand, so Patty gave it up.

At last the train started on again, and for a short time the trip was uneventful. Then the Italian gentleman looked at his watch, spoke to his wife, and rising, began to get his bags and coat from the rack.

"Why, they're going to get out," exclaimed Patty to Flo.

"So they are," said Flo. "I don't know why, but I somehow thought they were going all the way through to Venice. Well, I shall always remember the old lady's pleasant face."

The train was slowing down at a station, and the Italians shook hands with the girls in farewell.

"Signor?" said the old lady, looking at Patty, with a doubtful expression; "ritorno?"

"Oh, yes," said Patty; "he'll return. Si, si, signor ritorno soon."

It was not entirely intelligible, but the train had stopped, and the guard had flung the door open.

He announced some official information, which was as so much Greek to the two girls, then, with a final nod of good-by, the old lady clambered down the steps after her husband, and the guard slammed the door again.

"Parma," said Flo, reading the name on the station sign; "I suppose they are going after violets, don't you, Patty?"

"Yes, probably they'll pick big bunches along the roadside. But, Flo, we've lost our chaperon. It isn't at all the thing for two correct young ladies to be all alone in a railroad train at night."

"Well, your father will be back in a few minutes."

"Yes, of course he will. I'm not a bit afraid, but I know daddy won't like it. Still, it's his own fault. We couldn't help it, if our friend *would* get out to pick Parma violets.'"

"'Course we couldn't," said Flo.

CHAPTER XVI

AN EXCITING ADVENTURE

ANOTHER half hour went by, and Patty, looking at her watch, said, "Why, it's after nine o'clock! We will now eat our grapes. I meant to offer some to that dear old lady, but she preferred violets, so I had no chance."

The girls ate the grapes, and though they didn't refer to it, each secretly wished Mr. Fairfield would come back.

"It does seem queer," said Patty at last, "for father to stay so long away. But of course, he thinks the Orsinis are still with us, and if they were, I wouldn't give a thought to father's long absence."

"He's probably fallen asleep," said Flo.

"Of course he has! That's just it! His dinner and his smoke made him sleepy, and he dropped off before he knew it. Well, if he doesn't wake up before, he'll have to come and get us when we get to Venice."

"Maybe he'll sleep right through."

"Well, when we get to Venice, I'll get out then, and hunt up the Royal Danieli men, and they'll find him "

"How capable you Americans are! I don't mind confessing that I'm a bit scared."

"Pshaw! what is there to be scared at? We're as safe here as we can be. Nothing can harm us. The guards would look after us if there were any danger, but there isn't any."

"No, I suppose not," Flo agreed, but she spoke hesitatingly.

As for Patty, she was not really alarmed, but she couldn't helping wishing her father would come back. It would be all well enough in America or even in England; but alone on an Italian railway, where she couldn't make herself understood, and in a country where young ladies are allowed little or no unconventionality, she had secret misgivings. But it would never do to let Flo know she was troubled, so she said, gaily:

"Well, if daddy can have a nice long nap, so can I. Come, let's fold up our coats for pillows and drop asleep ourselves."

"Oh, no, Patty! It might be dangerous."

An Exciting Adventure

"Pooh, it's no more dangerous asleep then awake. I'm going to try it anyhow."

Patty made Flo comfortable first. She opened her dressing case, and taking out the Cologne water, bathed Flo's temples refreshingly. Then she folded her coat, and tucked it beneath her head, and said quietly:

"You needn't sleep, dear, if you don't want to, but you'll rest better that way."

Flo gave her a grateful smile and closed her eyes in order to rest them.

She was tired with the exertions of the day, and the long railway journey, and Patty was not surprised when, after a very few moments, she saw that Flo was, without doubt, fast asleep.

As for Patty Fairfield, she had no intention of going to sleep, and couldn't have done so, anyway. She felt the responsibility of the situation, for Snippy had left Flo in Mr. Fairfield's charge, and in his absence loyal Patty felt herself his representative. She sat upright, staring out of the window into the darkness or watching the doorway, where she expected every moment to see her father enter.

Bereft of even Flo's chatter, she grew more and more lonely, and only as the hands of her watch neared ten o'clock did she begin to

[237]

brighten up, on the knowledge that they must now soon reach Venice.

"But these trains are always late," she thought, "so I shan't hope to get there before half-past ten."

And then the time dragged along slowly. Half-past ten came, and no sign of her father. She had drawn the window curtain, but she pushed it aside, hoping to see the lights of Venice. Only a rushing darkness greeted her eyes. She looked at Flo. It seemed a pity to wake her, and yet Patty felt she couldn't endure this loneliness and suspense much longer. She knew the train should get in at ten, and surely a half hour was enough to allow for the usual tardiness.

But on went the hands of her little watch, and as it neared eleven Patty couldn't stand it any longer.

"Flo," she said, gently touching the sleeping girl, "Flo, dear." Flo moved uneasily, opened her eyes, closed them again, and was as sound asleep as ever.

"Well, I'll let her be," thought Patty, unselfishly. "She couldn't help any, and I don't know that there's anything to be helped. I suppose there's nothing wrong. What could

An Exciting Adventure

be? Father's asleep in the smoking-car, and Flo's asleep here, so I may as well sit patiently till we reach Venice, and then they'll have to wake up, whether they want to or not."

A guard came through the corridor, and looked in at the compartment door.

He said something in Italian, which Patty couldn't understand. But she showed him her watch, and said "Venice? stazione? when?"

She pointed to the hands, and partly comprehending, the guard took out his own watch and indicated that they would reach the *stazione* (station) at quarter to twelve.

"Train late?" said Patty, smiling, and still partly understanding, the guard said, "Si, signorina," bowed, and went away.

A little cheered at having had some one to speak to, even if for a most unsatisfactory conversation, Patty sat down again to wait. Her heart was quite light now, for it was nearly time to reach Venice, and then all would be well. At half-past eleven she wakened Flo.

"Get up, girlie," she cried. "We're almost to Venice, and you must tidy your hair and put your hat on."

Flo sat up, wide awake all at once. "Where's your father?" she said.

[239]

"He hasn't come back," said Patty, feeling somehow guilty under Flo's accusing glance, but determined to stand up for her father. "He must have fallen asleep, just as you did. I tried twice to wake you, but you slept like a log."

"And you've been all alone? Oh, Patty, I'm so sorry! Do forgive me!"

"Not at all, you sleepy child. It's all right, I see lights outside already. Here, put on your hat."

Flo rose and yawned, as she took her hat from Patty. They furbished up their toilets a bit, and soon were all ready to leave the train. Patty pushed the curtain up, and gazed out of the window.

"The lights are growing thicker now," she said; "we're almost in. I should think the porter would wake father up by this time. Well, I'm very sure nothing has happened to him."

Patty's decided statement gave Flo a clue that Patty *was* secretly afraid something *had* happened to her father, and as Flo had had such a fear all the time, she, too, stoutly denied it.

"Of course not! Nothing could happen to him. He's just asleep, as I was. I don't see

An Exciting Adventure

how you got me awake at all. Snippy has to throw cold water in my face to do it."

The train drew into the great station. There were many lights, but not many people about, which was doubtless because of the lateness of the hour.

The guard threw open the door of their compartment, and the two girls got out. Patty thought the guard looked at them a little curiously, and supposing he was desirous of a fee, she gave him some coins. He bowed, and still hovered near them.

"Where is the smoking-car?" asked Patty, but the guard knew not the strange word, and only shook his head.

"Flo," said Patty, looking about, "we'd better stand right here. When father gets out of his car, he'll come here for us. But didn't you think Venice had water streets? These are ordinary roads. And I see lots of omnibuses, but no gondolas."

"I suppose the water streets are only in the main part of the city," said Flo. "It does seem to be solid land all around the station. I can't see any water anywhere."

"Well, there must be some, somewhere. Flo, where *do* you suppose father is?"

[241]

"I don't know, Patty, and,—and, I'm—awfully frightened."

"Well, you just stop being frightened. I tell you everything is all right,—or will be, in a minute."

The crowd was moving along toward the entrance to the station, through which all the incoming passengers must go, and Patty reluctantly said, "We'd better go on into the station, Flo. We can't stand here, and father will surely find us there, if—if——"

Patty nearly broke down, for a sudden conviction had come to her that something serious *must* have happened to keep Mr. Fairfield from them now. The two girls, with their light luggage still in their hands, followed the crowd through the ticket gate.

"Biglietti," said the ticket man.

"I haven't any," said Patty, and without waiting to hear the man's surprised protest, Patty pushed Flo ahead of her, and they went on into the waiting-room of the station.

"Something has happened, Flo," she said, "something awful, perhaps,—but I can't imagine what it is. Now, we're alone, and unprotected in a strange land, and it's up to us to be brave and sensible. I shall take the gondola

An Exciting Adventure

or omnibus, or whatever goes to the Royal Danieli Hotel, and go right straight there. Then we can get somebody to look for father. But two young girls can do nothing, and we'd only waste time."

"You're splendid, Patty," said Flo, who was struggling hard to keep from crying. "I'm no good at all, but I'll do just as you say."

They went on to the platform, where a dozen or more omnibuses stood waiting, with their doors hospitably open. Names of hotels were in gilded letters over the doors, but Patty could not see the one she sought.

But at last she discovered an official, who seemed to be a sort of station agent or train-despatcher, and he had such a kindly, intelligent face that she addressed him:

"Do you speak English?" she said.

"Yes, miss, a little," he replied, looking at her with a questioning expression.

"Then please tell me where is the Royal Danieli Hotel?"

"It is in Venice, miss."

"Oh, yes, of course, I know it is in Venice; but I mean where is its omnibus? how can I get to it?"

"To get to it, you must go to Venice, ma'am."

"But I am in Venice!"

"No, ma'am, you are in Milan."

"What?" cried Patty, aghast at his words.

"This is Milan, ma'am."

"Are you,—are you quite sure?" Even in her bewildered horror, Patty realised the ludicrousness of this question.

"Perceive the signboard, ma'am." The man pointed to large-lettered sign, which unmistakably announced Milano.

"Flo," said Patty, in a scared, little voice, "I don't know what it means, but it seems we are in Milan instead of in Venice."

"Oh, Patty!" gasped Flo, as she clung desperately to Patty's arm; "what shall we do?"

"I don't know," said Patty, slowly; "it's a pretty serious thing for two girls to be alone in the middle of the night in a strange Italian city.

"But I took the train for Venice," said Patty to the man, and her tone had in it a faint tinge of accusation, though of course the man was in no way responsible.

"So, ma'am?" he replied, and in an instant Patty saw that he did not believe her statements, and that he was covertly laughing at them

An Exciting Adventure

"Come away, Flo," she said, sternly, and marched the now weeping girl into the station again.

"Listen, Flo," said Patty, her face assuming a very grave look. "We are in an awful predicament. Perhaps more awful than we know ourselves. We are in Milan, there's no doubt of that. That's why we didn't see any water or gondolas. Where father is I've no idea. Of course there was some mistake about the train. He may be gone on to Venice,— though I don't see how he could have done that without us,—or he may be in some other city. At any rate, he's quite as anxious about us as we can possibly be about ourselves. Now, I don't know what's going to happen to us, but I'm going to do the very best I can to prove that an American girl can take care of herself in an emergency. We won't speak to that man out there again; he's horrid, and he doesn't believe what we say. The ticket office is closed. There's no one reliable around but the drivers of those omnibuses. I shall appeal to them."

"Why don't you speak to some of the travellers?" asked Flo.

"Oh, you never can judge about them; and

[245]

they're mostly Italians anyway. Have you any money?"

"No; only a little change. Snippy carries the purse."

"Well, I've not very much, but I think I've enough. Now, come with me. Stand by me, and don't act one bit frightened. That's all you can do to help,—so *do it!*"

When Patty was face to face with a serious emergency, it always made her curt of speech, and her stern manner made Flo recover herself at once, so that it was two very dignified-looking young women who approached the drivers who, whip in hand, stood lined up along the platform.

Although they sometimes seemed eager to attract passengers, none of them asked the girls to get into their vehicles, and Patty went along until she came to one whose face she liked.

"Do you speak English?" she asked, as she looked at him coldly.

"Yes, madame."

"Which is the largest and best hotel in Milan, near the station?"

The driver pointed to a large hotel just across the road, scarcely a stone's throw from the station itself.

[246]

An Exciting Adventure

"The Palace Hotel, madame," he said respectfully.

"Where is its omnibus?"

"There, madame," and he pointed to a well-appointed vehicle standing near.

"Get in, Flo," said Patty, briefly. "Thank you," she added, turning to bestow a coin on the man.

"To the hotel," she then directed, as she got into the omnibus, and seated herself beside Flo.

"Oh, Patty!" said Flo, trembling, as she grasped Patty's hand. They were all alone in the omnibus, and in two minutes it was entering the driveway of the hotel.

"Be careful, now," said Patty, still sternly. "We're not out of the woods yet,—and if you cry or look distressed you'll spoil all I'm trying to do, and I'll not answer for the consequences. Now, brace up!"

Flo braced up, and as they alighted from the omnibus, Patty motioned for the porter to bring the bags and wraps.

She went directly to the desk, where the night attendant was.

"You speak English, of course?" she said.

"Yes, mademoiselle."

"We have had an accident,—a misfortune.

My friend and myself must stay here to-night. I wish to engage three communicating rooms, and I wish also the services of a maid,—I prefer an elderly woman,—who will remain with us through the night and will occupy the third room."

"Yes, mademoiselle." The man looked astonished, but Patty's quiet dignity, and Flo's impassive English stolidity, gave them an air of authority, which he was disinclined to ignore.

"Our large luggage was left on the train, owing to the—accident," went on Patty. "I will pay you fifty francs in advance and will settle the rest of the bill to-morrow. For the present it is imperative that we go to our rooms at once."

"Yes, mademoiselle," repeated the bewildered man. He was accustomed to American guests, but this was a new type.

He rang a bell, he despatched one or two messengers, he called a porter, and in a few moments Patty saw her bag and cloak carried by, the elevator door thrown open, and a pleasant-faced matronly woman coming toward them.

"This is Mrs. Ponderby, mademoiselle. She is one of our linen-keepers, but she is English,

[248]

and most trusty and capable, so I offer you her services."

Patty almost fell into the arms of the kind-looking woman, she was so glad to see her, but she only shook hands and said, " I am glad to have your services, Mrs. Ponderby,—come, let us go upstairs."

CHAPTER XVII

THE OTHER SIDE OF THE STORY

WHEN they were safely in their rooms, behind locked doors, Flo threw herself into Mrs. Ponderby's motherly arms and wept as hard as she could, which was really pretty hard.

Patty stood by, looking at her. It had been a nerve strain for Patty, and now the reaction was coming on. Her lip quivered, and she said: " It isn't fair of you, Flo, to take up all Mrs. Ponderby; I'm worse off than you are, for I don't know but what my father is killed in some awful railroad smash-up."

" He c-couldn't be," said Flo, sobbing still; " there c-couldn't have been a smash-up on that train, unless we had known ab-bout it ! "

" Well, I don't know where father is, any-how; and he doesn't know where I am ! "

Then Patty burst into real sobs, and the kind-hearted Englishwoman was at her wits' end to know what to do with these two strange mid-

[250]

night visitors. But she rose nobly to the occasion.

"There, there, my lambs," she said, soothingly, "you can tell me all about it presently. But first let us get comfortable. Take off your dusty travelling frocks, and—have you any dressing-gowns?"

"No," said Patty; "only just our night things. I've only my furnished toilet bag, and Flo hasn't even that."

"Never mind, dearie; we'll improvise dressing jackets out of these big bath towels. Now shall I ring the bell and order a bite of supper? A sandwich now,—and a cup of coffee?"

"Not coffee," said Flo, rousing herself a bit, "it keeps me awake. Let's have chocolate."

"Yes," said Patty; "hot chocolate and chicken sandwiches."

"And t-tongue," put in sobbing Flo.

"And jam," said Patty, almost smiling, now.

"Yes, yes,—assorted sandwiches, and nice hot cocoa."

Mrs. Ponderby rang the bell and gave the order, and by the time the tray was brought, she had helped the girls to bathe their faces, and had deftly pinned huge bath towels round their shoulders in a very good imitation of dressing-sacques. And not until they were sipping their second cups of cocoa, and had made way with a goodly number of the little sandwiches, did she say, "Now tell me all about it."

Patty told the whole story of their trip from Florence—and how her father had left them to go to the smoking-car for half an hour, and they had not seen him again.

"Do you suppose brigands attacked him?" asked Patty, her eyes wide open with fear and wonder.

"No, dearie; not that. But it's a strange story you tell, and I can think of only one explanation. Rest here, and don't think about it for five minutes, till I return."

Mrs. Ponderby hurried away, and was back again in less than five minutes.

"It's as I thought," she said. "That train you took from Florence is really in two sections. That is, half of its cars are for Venice, and half for Milan. At Bologna, the train is divided and sent in two directions. You see, Bologna is the southern point of a triangle. From there, one travels northeast to Venice, or northwest to Milan. Those two cities form the other two points of the triangle. So, when the train was

[252]

divided at Bologna, some cars, including the one your father was in, went on to Venice; while other cars, including the one you were in, branched off to Milan, and here you are."

Patty cogitated on this.

"Then," she said, "when father tried to return to our car, our car wasn't there."

"Exactly; it had already been detached and sent to Milan."

"Could father find this out?"

"Oh, yes; from the train guard. But he should have taken his seats in a car for Venice in the first place."

"We were put in our places by the man from the hotel in Florence," declared Patty, "so it wasn't father's fault at all."

"Then you should all have changed cars at Bologna, and taken seats in a Venice car."

"Yes," agreed Patty; "that's where the mistake occurred. And all because neither father nor I understand Italian. I daresay the guard announced that,—he was shouting all sorts of directions,—but of course, I didn't understand him, and father didn't either. And, too, I daresay father was asleep. You know, we all thought we were going directly through to Venice, so we spent the evening as pleasantly

[253]

as we could, never dreaming we had to change cars or anything."

"Yes, that explains it all, Miss Fairfield, and you have proved yourself a most sensible and capable young woman to manage as well as you have done. An Italian city is no place for two girls alone."

"I know it, Mrs. Ponderby. Don't think I didn't realise the seriousness of it all. But I did the best I could. You know I am an American." Patty said this so proudly that the Englishwoman gave her a look of admiration.

"True," she said; "an English girl might not have been so brave."

"No, I wasn't," confessed Flo; "I depended on Patty, for I knew she could take care of things if anybody could."

"But," said Patty, suddenly; "think of father! When he tried to return to us, and couldn't find us, what *do* you suppose he did!"

"He couldn't do anything," said Mrs. Ponderby, "except to find out that you had gone on to Milan."

"He couldn't find that out," said Patty, slowly, "unless he found some one who could explain it to him in English. You see, it's quite

[254]

complicated, with the divided train and all. And besides, father was nearly frantic with worry about us."

"Yes, he must have been," said Mrs. Ponderby, gravely. "But he could do nothing at all, except to go on to Venice. He's there now, of course. Shall you not telegraph him that you are safe?"

"Indeed I will!" cried Patty. "Bless you for suggesting it. I seem to have lost my wits. Oh, Flo, what *will* Snippy say when father gets there without us?"

"She'll be in an awful way," said Flo. "And Nan will be 'most crazy. Oh, Patty, they're really having a worse time of it than we are, now. Just think! They don't know where we are, even!"

"Yes," said Patty, thinking. "Father must know we came on to Milan."

"No, he doesn't; he may think we got off at some other station. You know the train stopped three or four times. Or he may think we got off at Bologna and staid there."

"That's so," agreed Patty. "Well, he knows me well enough to know that I'll do the best I can; and I do believe, Flo, that he feels it a worse responsibility to have lost you than me!"

[255]

"If he doesn't, it won't be Snip's fault," said Flo, grimly. "She'll give him a waxing, I'll warrant."

"It wasn't father's fault," said Patty, staunchly. "That hotel man ought to have told us to change cars at Bologna. Nice railroad management! Well, I'll telegraph at once, for he can't very well telegraph to us, when he doesn't know where we are." Mrs. Ponderby brought blanks, and Patty wrote a long telegram:

"We are nicely fixed at the Palace Hotel, with comfortable rooms, and a dear English duenna. Send Snippy for us as soon as possible, and we will gladly rejoin you.

"Patty and Flo."

Mrs. Ponderby bustled away to send the telegram, and then returned to tuck her charges into bed.

"It's lucky you know the hotel your people are staying at in Venice," she said; "and now go quietly to sleep, for you've done all you can. But I doubt me if your poor father is sleeping much."

"Or Snippy," said Flo.

[256]

"Or Nan," said Patty. "We've got to do the sleeping for all the family, to-night, Flo; so let's get about it."

Knowing she had done all she could in the matter, and thoroughly worn out with the journey and the after excitement, Patty turned on her pillow, and was soon sound asleep.

But far from sleep at that moment was Mr. Fairfield. The poor man was passing through an awful experience. As Patty had surmised, he had dropped asleep in the smoking-car, but he had dozed only for a few moments, and, of course, had no thought other than that his two young charges were in their cosy compartment, with the elderly and kind Italian couple.

Then, soon after leaving Bologna, and all unsuspecting that the train had been divided, he started to return to Patty and Flo, and found to his amazement that that car with several others had been disconnected at Bologna. Mr. Fairfield was stunned. He found an official who could talk fairly good English, and laid the case before him. But there was nothing to be done. Although a clever and resourceful man, Mr. Fairfield felt that his hands were tied. He knew Patty was on the train for Milan, but he could not guess at what station she would get off, if indeed she had not left the train at Bologna.

For the moment his anxiety for the girls' safety was lost in an endeavour to think of some way to get into communication with them. There was nothing to be gained by getting off the train himself, and yet he hated to go on to Venice without them. But to return to Bologna would be a wild-goose chase, and, too, there was no train back for several hours. He felt sure that Patty would be brave and sensible, but he could not imagine what course she would pursue, and he well knew that real dangers beset the two lonely girls.

So he wrote telegrams which he put off to be sent at the next station. He sent one to Bologna, to be called out in the station, on the chance of Patty's being there. He sent duplicates to Milan, and to every intervening station at which the train stopped. He felt little hope that any of these would really reach Patty, but he could think of no other plan. Had he been sure she would go through to Milan, he would have gone directly there himself, but so few and inconvenient were the trains that this plan was dismissed. And, too, he must go on to

[258]

The Other Side of the Story

Venice, where Nan and Snippy were awaiting them.

An awful dread of Snippy's reception of his news filled Mr. Fairfield with consternation, but, as he thought, since his own daughter was lost, as well as Snippy's young charge, his own grief was as great as hers. And try as he would to rely on Patty's bravery, and capability in an emergency, he shuddered to think of those two girls, carried swiftly through the night, alone, unprotected, and wondering why he did not return to them.

It was some comfort to realise that the kind old Italian pair were with them. Had Mr. Fairfield known that they left the train at Parma, he would have been racked with a worse anxiety. But he hoped that wherever they all were, the quartette were together, and his faith in the kindly old people was such that he felt sure they would look after the girls some way.

So he arrived in Venice a sad, crushed man, and stepped into the beautiful gondola sent to meet him by the Royal Danieli Hotel without a glance at the canals, the bridges the buildings, and the lights, that are so fascinating to the newcomers to Venice.

With his head bowed in his hands he made the

[259]

trip to the hotel, and went in to find Nan and Snippy awaiting him in the reception room.

"Where are the girls?" cried Nan, gaily, as she greeted her husband, little thinking of anything more serious than that they had paused outside to look at the scene, or something like that.

"Have you our own rooms, all right?" said Mr. Fairfield, abruptly.

"Yes, Fred," said Nan, wondering at his manner.

"Then let us go to them at once," he said, and so grave was his face that, without another word, Nan led the way, and the three went up the magnificent ducal staircase, to their rooms on the next floor. Here, in a few frank statements, Mr. Fairfield told his story. As he concluded, Snippy's eyes flashed fire, and she glared at him.

"You have lost Miss Flo!" she exclaimed. "I trusted her to your care!"

"Mrs. Postlethwaite," said Mr. Fairfield, and the fact of his using her name made Snippy pause to listen, "when my own daughter is also lost, you cannot fairly say I betrayed a trust. I admit my culpability in the matter, but I think in this very grave emergency we must all

[260]

do what we can to find the girls, and not give way to useless recrimination."

"I think so, too," said Nan, taking her husband's hand, "and, Mrs. Postlethwaite, while I sympathise with you regarding Flo, you must also realise what we are suffering regarding Patty; and though you are Flo's guardian and governess,—yet Patty is our daughter."

Snippy's sense of justice came to her rescue, and she said, more quietly:

"Forgive me, Mr. Fairfield; I was so shocked and upset at Miss Flo's disappearance, I quite overlooked Miss Patty. I won't admit that you are in a worse case than I, for I am responsible to Miss Flo's mother, while Miss Patty is your own child. But I appreciate the situation, and we will work together to do all we can to get the children back as soon as possible."

"That's the sensible Snippy that you are!" said Mr. Fairfield, as he heartily clasped her hand; "but, alas! I cannot think of anything to do. It doesn't seem right to refer the case to the police, as I can't help thinking the girls are safe somewhere with the Italian lady and gentleman, and if I know my Patty, she'll telegraph me as soon as she can. Thank Heaven she knows our Venice address. Hard as it is, I think the only thing we can do now is to wait until morning."

The others agreed to this. and so they all went to bed, though not to sleep.

CHAPTER XVIII

VENICE AT LAST

VERY early the next morning, Snippy, who had fallen into a light doze, was awakened by a tapping at her door.

Hastily flinging on her dressing-gown, she opened the door to see Mr. Fairfield standing there with a smiling face that betokened good news. He waved a telegram at her, and exclaimed: "The girls are all right, Snippy. We may congratulate each other!"

"Thank Heaven!" cried the delighted woman, and then her eyes eagerly devoured the telegram Patty had sent.

"Bless her heart!" she said; "she's a good girl, is Miss Patty, Mr. Fairfield. And to think of those two dear children alone in Milan! How soon can I start?"

Mr. Fairfield smiled at her ready acceptance of Patty's suggestion, and replied:

"You must get your breakfast first. The girls are all right now, you know. I've tele-

[263]

graphed them that we've received their message and will send for them. You can reach them by noon, I think, and have them back here before sunset. I'll go for them, if you prefer."

But Snippy declared herself quite willing to go, so, after an early breakfast, she set out for Milan.

Accustomed to travelling, she did not mind the journey at all, and in her gladness at Flo's safety, she was once again her own staid, sensible self.

She reached the hotel duly, paid the bills the girls had incurred, gave Mrs. Ponderby a generous gift from Mr. Fairfield, and many earnest thanks from them all.

" It's so nice that you can't scold me, Snippy," remarked Flo, after they were in the train for Venice; " somehow, I think you'd like to scold somebody, and you know that I wasn't a bit to blame. You daren't scold Mr. Fairfield; Patty deserves only praise; so, poor thing, you've nobody to berate, have you? "

" I blame myself, Miss Flo," said Snippy, primly, " that I ever let you out of my sight."

" Oh, well, Snips, all's well that ends well, and we'll have a booful time in Venice."

Flo never took Snippy very seriously, so the

[264]

two girls gave themselves up to enjoyment of their journey, and looked forward eagerly to their arrival in Venice at last.

Patty sprang from the train straight into her father's arms, and the welcoming kiss he gave her told her how glad he was to have her safely beside him once more.

" And now," said Nan, after they had all welcomed each other, " we've just time for a leisurely water trip back to the hotel. This is our gondola, the flowers are in honour of your arrival."

Nan pointed to a graceful craft which was waiting for them. It was a well-shaped, freshly-painted gondola, and its black sides and shining metal made it quite distinct from the more dingy affairs all around. Also, the gondolier wore a resplendent sash of bright colours, and his handsome Italian face was good-natured and smiling.

" It's ours," said Nan, proudly; " I mean, while we're here. I picked it out yesterday, and it's the finest gondola in all Venice, eh, Donatello ? "

The gondolier showed his white teeth in an assenting grin, though he scarcely understood the question.

"It's angelic!" declared Patty, as she stepped in. "And the lovely dry carpet! I thought of course the bottom of a gondola was of a wet and sloppy nature."

"You goose!" cried Nan. "But sit down, Patty, and drink it all in."

"What! the canal?" cried Patty, but she sat down and looked about her with that awed thrill that the first sight of Venice brings to all good Americans.

It was not far from the sunset hour, and the cabin of the gondola had been removed, so they could see the gay scenes all about.

"It's perfect!" said Patty, as she gazed delightedly at sea, and sky, and buildings. "It's all my fancy painted it, only I didn't think it would be a bit like this!"

"I did," said Flo. "It's exactly like the postcards of it, only bigger."

"So it is," said Nan; "I recognised that myself. And the more you see of it, the more you'll love it."

Then they came to the Rialto Bridge, and Patty wanted to get out and walk across it, but her father said there wasn't time then, she must wait till the next day. So she and Flo just sat still and drifted calmly along, both feeling that the scene was too lovely even for words of appreciation.

On they swept, round the great curves of the Grand Canal, and now and then the gondolier sang out the name of a house or a church they were passing.

"He's worse than an elevated road conductor," said Patty. "I can't make out a word he says; but then I don't want to. I don't care to-night which church is which, and if the Borgias had lived in Browning's house, I should make no objection."

"Well, here's the Piazzetta," said her father; "you must learn this, as you'll spend a lot of time here. It leads to the Piazza of St. Mark, and is the meeting place of all Venice."

"Then I suppose you'll call St. Mark's the meeting-house," said Patty; "it sounds provincial to me."

"Don't be disrespectful," said her father; "before two days have passed, you'll be everlastingly making tracks for the Piazza."

"Not I," said Patty; "I expect to live in a gondola. Can't I have one all to myself, Father? Just for Flo and me, I mean. You and Nan will be always wanting this one."

"We'll get another, if you like, girlie. But I

won't let you and Flo go alone in it. Snippy and I are to accompany you always hereafter. Why, first thing you knew you'd be back in Milan! But here we are at our hotel."

The gondola turned softly round into a side canal which led past the steps of the Hotel Royal Danieli, and they all stepped out.

Patty soon learned the knack of gracefully balancing herself as she disembarked, but Flo was nervously uncertain of her steps.

"I don't like the wabbly things!" she exclaimed, as she almost slipped upon the wet lower step of the hotel entrance.

"Oh," said Nan, "you'll get used to bobbling around in a day or two. They're really lots easier to get into than your London 'buses."

"Indeed they are," said Patty. "I love 'em. I'm going to try to have water introduced into the New York streets. It's the nicest sort of road."

Then they all went into the beautiful hotel, which used to be the palace of a great Italian family.

The elaborate architecture and decorations, and many of the magnificent pieces of furniture were still there, and the grand staircase, with lights and palms and flowers, was an impressive sight.

Venice at Last

"Well," said Patty, "this makes 'the grandeur that was Rome' look like three United States dimes!"

"Oh, Patty!" cried Nan, "how can you use slang in Venice?"

But the allusion was lost on Flo and Snippy, who knew little of American jests.

Their rooms looked out on the Grand Canal, and there was a wide board sidewalk between the hotel and the water.

This was crowded with people promenading up and down, both Italians and foreigners.

"Well," said Patty to Flo, through the open door of their adjoining rooms. "Will you look at that! If it isn't like the board walk at Atlantic City!"

Flo had never seen Atlantic City, but she, too, was fascinated by the brilliant pageant, and the two girls sat in the window, gazing out, quite forgetting that they had been told to change their frocks for dinner. Nan came in, trailing her pretty white draperies.

"Why, girls, haven't you begun to dress?" she said. "You must hurry. We want to dine and then go Venicing by moonlight."

"Ooh, ee!" cried Patty; "I'll be attired in two minutes. Hurry up, Flo. Snippy will hook you, and Nan will help me, won't you, ducky stepmother o' mine?"

"Yes, if you'll fly 'round," said Nan, laughing, as Patty shook down her sunny tangle of curls, and then shook it up again, and twisted a white ribbon through it.

"What shall I wear, Nan? Open my trunk and get out anything you like."

"This light green thing, with silver lace on it, comes first," said Nan, diving into Patty's trunk.

"All right, I'll wear that. Do I want a hat?"

"No; your hair looks lovely. Here's a white and silver scarf you can take, to wear out after dinner."

"All right, honey. Here, hook me up, please; where's my priceless string of Roman pearl beads?"

"Here they are, but I think your pink coral prettier."

"Not a bit, you colour-blind infant. These pure white pearls, warranted pure white wax, are the only thing to wear with this green and silver symphony."

"Yes, you're right," said Nan, as Patty, with toilette completed, stood fair and sweet for inspection. "You always do wear just the right things, Patty."

"So do you," was the affectionate reply, and arm in arm they went down the great staircase.

The party all met in one of the drawing-rooms, and Mr. Fairfield surveyed his pretty wife and daughter with the pride he always felt in their charm and attractiveness.

Flo, too, looked dainty and well-dressed, and Snippy, in her black satin, was a perfect model of an English duenna.

"Come on," said Nan, to her husband, "let us go in to dinner."

"Wait a moment," said Mr. Fairfield, looking at his watch. "It isn't quite time."

"Yes, it is, Daddy," said Patty, who was darting about in her excitement; now looking out of the window,—now admiring the appointments indoors. "Lots of people have gone to the dining-room."

"And here are lots more to go," said her father, triumphantly, as three smiling young men, resplendent in evening clothes, made a simultaneous and sudden appearance.

"Why, you blessed boys!" cried Patty, as with outstretched hands and shining eyes she greeted Peter Homer, Floyd Austin, and Caddy Oram.

"Rejoiced at being reunited to their long-lost

friends, the young men rolled their eyes in ec
stasy," said Austin, and as he nudged the others,
they all three struck an attitude and rolled their
eyes ridiculously toward the ceiling.

"Oh, I'm so *glad* to see you!" exclaimed Patty;
"how dear of you to come while we're here!
Isn't it, Flo?"

"Yes, awfully jolly," said Flo, who was glad
to see the boys, but could not be so spontaneous
of manner as Patty.

"Now we'll go to dinner," said Mr. Fairfield,
and then it came out that he had known the
three young men were in Venice, and had invited them to dinner that night as a surprise
to Patty and Flo.

It was a merry dinner, indeed. Snippy and
the elder Fairfields were so glad to have the girls
safely with them again that they were fairly
beaming with joy.

And as for the five young people, they were
just bubbling over with the merriment of youth
and happiness.

"Have you had a good time all through
Italy?" asked Peter Homer, of Patty.

"Oh, yes, indeed it has been the pleasurablest
pleasure trip I could imagine. Everything has
gone right,—except," she paused suddenly, as

she remembered the episode of the night before. But she resolved not to bring up the subject then, so she went on, saying, " except that of course we were lonely in Florence without you three, and the other Wonderers. But we can wonder through Venice together, and oh, won't it be lovely! I haven't seen Venice at all yet, except just the row up from the station."

" Venice is Heaven and water." said Peter Homer, and Austin droned out:

" Having made a pretty good epigram, he waited for the applause due him."

" He'll get it, too," said Patty, softly clapping her hands. " Venice is Heaven and water. I've already noticed it, and should have said it myself, if I'd thought of it."

" Never mind," said Floyd, consolingly; " you can say it to the next bunch of people you meet, and then you'll get some nice applause."

As soon as dinner was over, Mr. Fairfield invited the whole party to go for a moonlight row. He had engaged a barca, which is larger than a gondola, and it held them all comfortably.

As they glided out into the Grand Canal, Patty fairly held her breath at the marvel of the scene. The moon, not far from full, sent silver-crested ripples along the surface of the water. The strange and wonderful buildings loomed weirdly against the sky. On the bridges and quays were sparkling lights and merry people; while ever and again other silent, dark gondolas glided swiftly past their own craft.

"Oh," said Patty,—"oh!" Realising the beauty of the whole effect, even Floyd Austin refrained from making his nonsensical speeches, and all sat silent and absorbed, as the gondoliers plashed their oars.

"Sing, Patty," said Nan, at last.

"Yes, do," said everybody, but Patty said:

"No, that would be out of the picture. Ask the gondoliers to sing."

"No," said Peter Homer, quietly. "You sing first, Patty, and then we'll have them sing a barcarole."

"I'd do anything to hear them sing a barcarole. What is it? It sounds like something to eat."

"Patty!" cried Flo, "don't talk of eating in this enchanted place!"

"Well, I won't," said Patty, good-naturedly. "What shall I sing?"

"Some pretty little sentimental thing," suggested Floyd. "Soft and low, you know."

"I don't know much sentimental music," said Patty, "but I'll sing *Secrets.*"

So as the boat silently sped along the water, eluding other boats here and there, guided by the skilful gondoliers, Patty's sweet voice sang softly, to a gentle, charming air:

"SECRETS

"Away and away from the busy town,
  Soft on the sea the stars shine down;
    And nobody knows of the stars and the sea,
    But Mine and Me.

"Away and away the wind breathes low,
  The branches are waving to and fro;
    And nobody knows of the wind in the tree,
    But Mine and Me.

"Away and away in a far somewhere
  The roses are red and sweet and fair;
    And nobody knows of a rose that may be,
    But Mine and Me.

"Away and away on a blue lagoon,
  Shines softly,—softly,—the silvery moon;
    And nobody knows of the wavelets' plea,
    But Mine and Me."

[275]

The last strains rang out across the water, and as Patty's voice ceased, a whispered " Brava ! " was heard from one of the gondoliers.

" Brava, indeed," said Peter Homer. " Thank you, Patty, for a, great pleasure. Now, the gondoliers shall sing for you in return."

They were easily induced to do so, and their Italian songs kept time to the rippling dip of their trained touch of the oar.

" I'm in the seventh heaven," murmured Patty, as a song came to an end.

" And water," supplemented Caddy. " Don't forget your new-found epigram."

" But I'm not in the water," rejoined Patty, laughing. " What is that church? You may as well make up your minds to tell me every time, for I'm not going to try to remember. I don't think one ought to remember anything in Venice, but just drift along and look and wonder."

" That is the Santa Maria della Salute," said her father.

" Indeed ! " said Patty, saucily. " And why are the statues around its dome all on bicycles ? "

" They're not ! Patty, I'm ashamed of you ! "

" Well, they look as if they are ? Don't they, Caddy ? "

"Exactly. But they are bicycles only by moonlight; in broad daylight they are quite different. I'll bring you to-morrow, and show you."

They rowed around in desultory fashion, enjoying the evening, now and then waxing merry and talking nonsense, and again, growing pensive, as the moonlight demanded.

At last they stopped at the Piazzetta, and Mr. Fairfield took the party to the Piazza for ices.

"Oh," cried Patty, as she saw the gay scene; banners flying, a band playing, lights sparkling; people walking about, and sitting at small tables; "oh, why didn't we come here sooner! Moonlight and water pale beside this fairyland! Oh,—ooh!"

Patty almost danced about in glee. She loved gay sound and sight, and this was so novel and so brilliant it delighted her beyond measure.

"There, there, child," said her father; "calm your transports. Remember this is your first night in Venice. You must learn to get used to it."

"I will," said Patty, rapturously. "I'd love to. Just give me time!"

Peter Homer was watching her with an intense interest in her naïve enjoyment.

"You are seeing Italy the way I want you to," he said, as they all sat down at the little tables.

"Is this your Venice?" asked Patty, glancing about at the crowds.

"Yes, it's all my Venice. I mean the way we're seeing it to-night. The rapid impressions of the moonlight and water, followed by this gay and lively scene, *is* Venice. And to-morrow—many to-morrows, I shall show you other sides of the city's charm, until you can mingle all your memories into a perfect picture of the whole."

"You are so good to me," said Patty; "I like to have you take such an interest in my sight-seeing."

"And I like to take it, but suppose you see if you can take an interest in these ices and cakes that are approaching us."

"I just guess I can!" said Patty. "I'm as hungry as if I were in New York!"

CHAPTER XIX

PIGEONS AND POETRY

THE days in Venice rippled by so happily that Patty couldn't realise how fast they were going. Their own party was usually joined by some or all of the three young men, whose hotel was not far away.

Although it was in early November, the weather was only pleasantly crisp, and during much of the day it was warm, with an Indian summer haze in the air.

"What mood this morning, oh, Fair One with golden locks?" said Floyd Austin, as he came into the hotel and found Patty idly sitting in the reading-room.

"Aimless and amiable," she replied, smiling at him.

"Ha! 'tis a mood that well befitteth mine own. Let's go and feed the pigeons."

"All right, let's. Flo's having her hair washed, and Nan and father have gone off somewhere, so I'm glad to have somebody to play with."

"H'm—a doubtful compliment,—but I'll forgive you. Get your hat."

Patty flew for her hat and cloak, and paused to look in at Flo's door.

"I'm going to the Piazza," she said, "with Floyd, to feed the pigeons. Come on over, when your hair is dry."

"All right, I will," said Flo, as intelligibly as she could through masses of wet locks.

Patty ran on downstairs, and joined Floyd, and together they sauntered along toward the Piazza.

"I can't imagine being busy in Venice," said Patty, looking at the idlers of all castes that were everywhere about. "I don't see how they ever get anything done."

"They don't," said Floyd; "nobody has anything to do,—or if he does, he doesn't do it. Let's cross over here, and look in the shop windows."

"Yes; I love to look in windows. And I want to get some silver things for my memory chain. What shall I get?"

"Absurd question! Of course you must get a little silver gondola,—there's a beauty, see it?

And a Lion of St. Mark; and a pigeon,—oh, Venice has so many typical toys,—it's too easy!"

"Yes, so it is. I had hard work to find anything in Florence, though."

They went into several shops, one after another, and Patty bought little trinkets to hang on her chain, and other souvenirs beside.

"What a very long tail the lion has," she said, as she looked at some bronze paper-weights that were models of the famous beast.

"Yes; it would make a lovely poem. 'The Lion of St. Mark's, with his very long tail,'—— Go on."

"'Wept a whole week 'cos he wasn't a whale,'" said Patty, promptly; for making verses was one of their favourite games; "go on, yourself."

"'For,' he said, 'here is water all over the place,——'"

"'And I'm sure I could swim with exquisite grace.'"

"Good for you, Patty; you had the rhyming lines, that's hardest. I'll take 'em next time."

"All right; here you are! 'A poor little pigeon was hungry one day——'"

"'And he hoped Floyd and Patty would come by that way.'"

" ' As they were approaching, he spied them afar,——' "

" And he said, ' What a fine-looking couple they are ! ' "

" Oh, Floyd, how vain you are ! "

" Speak for yourself ! You don't seem to object to your own share of the pigeon's opinion."

" Of course I don't. Come on; after that compliment from the pigeon, we must give him a whole heap of corn."

" How will you know which pigeon's the one ? "

" Oh, I can tell by the expression in his eye. Get some corn, please; a lot of it."

As they neared the east end of the Piazza, they had to step carefully, lest they tread on the hundreds of pigeons which crowded their feet, eager for corn.

Floyd bought the corn from the vendors near by, and handed a parcel to Patty.

" Now I see why they call these cornucopias," she said, taking the paper horn that held the yellow kernels. " I suppose this shaped twist of paper was first used to hold corn for St. Mark's pigeons."

" Of course it was. Somebody had a corner

in corn, and so he had to invent cornucopias to hold it all."

"What nonsense you *do* talk," said Patty, giggling at his foolishness. "There, that's the pigeon who has been watching and waiting for us."

She pointed to a very large, fat bird, who stood with a pompous air, a little aloof from the rest. His neck and breast shone in the sunlight, and the iridescent gleams shimmered with every graceful movement.

"He's proud," said Patty, "and won't deign to coax for corn, like the others."

"He's stuffed, you mean! I don't believe he could eat another grain unless it was pushed down his throat for him. The last three letters of his name should be pronounced silent."

"P-i-g. Oh! he isn't any such thing! He's simply more polite than the rest. Watch him eat."

Patty threw some corn to him, and the pigeon ate it with a quiet dignity, but they soon realised that any more might give him a fit of apoplexy, so they fed it all to the others.

It was great fun to watch the pigeons, and especially to watch the little children feed them. Babies of two or three years would timidly throw a grain of corn, and then run squealing away from the commotion it produced.

"Let's go and see something," said Patty, when their corn was all gone and she had grown tired of sitting still.

"All right, but don't go far. Shall it be the Cathedral or the Doge's Palace?"

"The Palace. I want to go into those horrible dungeons once more before I leave Venice."

So they loitered slowly through the rooms of the Palace, and then crossed the Bridge of Sighs.

"I always smile when I cross this bridge," said Patty, "because the poor old bridge has had so many weeping people cross it, that I'm sure it's glad of the change."

"Of course it is. We ought to stand here and grin for a week, to make up for the groans and wails with which these poor old walls must be saturated. But I say, Patty, here's a small party of tourists with a guide. Let's join them to go through the dungeons."

As visitors were not allowed in the prisons without being officially conducted, this was a good plan, and once again Patty made the tour of the dark, dismal holes, where prisoners were confined, tortured, and put to death.

Pigeons and Poetry

"Ugh!" said Floyd, as they at last came out into the sunlight again, "how can you want to see those horrors, when you can look at this instead!"

They stood on the sidewalk in front of the Palace—and saw, spread out before them, the blue water, sparkling with gold ripples; the blue sky, flecked with soft, white clouds; and all the beautiful vista of Venice.

"I don't know," said Patty, thoughtfully. "I didn't enjoy it as a spectacle, but I wanted a memory of those prison cells, as well as of the beautiful things. Oh, here comes Flo,—isn't she the beautiful thing, with her raving locks all freshly washed and ironed!"

Flo came smiling toward them, followed by the inevitable Snippy, who, having had her lesson, never let her young mistress stir without her. But nobody minded, for Snippy was an agreeable, if not very merry companion, and, too, she had a kind habit of effacing herself from the conversation, when the young people wanted to chatter nonsense.

The last evening of their stay in Venice, Mr. Fairfield gave a water-party. They had made a number of pleasant acquaintances, and these,

[285]

in addition to their own immediate party, made about two score.

Several gondolas had been engaged, and these the gondoliers, with rival pride, had decorated gaily.

Lanterns swung from the cabins, and flowers and gay streamers gave the craft a festal air. The gondoliers, too, wore brilliant garb, and as the fleet floated away from the hotel, it was a picturesque sight.

Patty wore a fluffy, light blue dress, and a long, light blue cloak, lined with white silk, which enveloped her from head to foot. It had an ermine collar, for the evenings were growing chill; and a dainty blue toque, edged with ermine, sat saucily on Patty's gold curls.

"You look a picture!" said Peter Homer, as he handed her into a gondola.

"An old master?" asked Patty, smiling gaily at him.

"No, indeed. Rather like one of your new American masters, who draw such fascinating girls."

"Thank you for a subtle compliment," said Patty, comfortably arranging herself on the red-cushioned seat. "You may sit beside me for that."

"Thank you. My effort was not in vain, then. Virtue, like Venice, is its own reward."

The fleet started and made a delightful pre-arranged trip along the Grand Canal, and through many of the most picturesque smaller canals. Their gondolas kept together as much as possible, and gay chat was tossed across from one to another. Returning, they stopped at the Piazza, and sat for a time, or strolled about, listening to the music of the band. Then all walked the short distance to the Royal Danieli, and gathered in one of the smaller ballrooms, which Mr. Fairfield had engaged.

Some musicians played, and a delightful dance ensued. Patty always enjoyed dancing, and treated quite impartially the many would-be partners who begged to be favoured.

"Isn't she a wonder?" said Caddy Oram to Peter Homer, as Patty waltzed by with Floyd.

"The most sunshiny girl I have ever seen," said Peter, gazing at graceful Patty, who smiled back at him over Floyd's shoulder.

The dance ended all too soon, and then the guests were ushered to the dining-room, where a supper was spread on small tables.

"It would be a lovely party," said Patty, "if

it weren't to celebrate our last evening in Venice. That makes me sad."

"It makes me heart-broken," said Floyd; "Venice without you is as dust and ashes. My soul is as a crushed cauliflower! Alack-a-day, and wae's me!"

"Come along with us," said Patty, ignoring his show of grief. "The Venetians will let you off, I'm sure."

"That may be, madame. But I've affairs of more importance than trailing an American girl all over the map of Europe."

"I'd like to follow the trail," said Peter Homer, "but I've been summoned back to London, and 'England expects.'"

"I wish I could take you all home with me," said Patty, enthusiastically; "you're a lovely bunch of boys, and you'd grace any country."

"Thank ye, ma'am," said Floyd, as they all bowed politely.

And when they took leave, the three declared that they would be on hand next morning to conduct the Fairfield party to the railway station.

True to their word, they appeared in ample time to escort the travellers.

Several gondolas were required, and it somehow happened that Peter Homer and Patty, with one or two trunks, occupied one of them alone.

"This is as it should be," he said, in a tone of satisfaction. "I'm glad to be with you as you see the last of Venice. But I hope we shall meet here again sometime."

"I hope so," said Patty, carelessly. "I suppose I shall come again,—everybody does,—but will you be here then?"

"Yes, if you call me. I'll have to be here to guide your impressions in the right channels."

"Canals, you mean," said Patty, laughing at his serious face.

"Very well, canals. You are an apt pupil. Tell me, now, what is Venice like this morning?"

Patty looked around at the glowing scene. The autumn sunshine, the crisp, fine air, the beauty of form and colour everywhere. Then she said:

"Liquid sunlight, streaming down, as if strained through a golden sieve."

"Rubbish!" cried Floyd, as, in another gondola, he drifted alongside. "Where'd you get that padded plush sentiment, Patty?"

"Isn't it poetic?" she said, turning to Peter, with a look of mock anxiety.

"No," he replied, "it's forced and ridiculous, and you know it."

"Yes, so I do," said Patty, her face dimpling into smiles. "But you always make me feel as if I ought to feel that way about Venice."

"Oh, well, you're so foolishly young, yet. But you'll get over it. Meantime, will you accept a tiny souvenir of the Grand Canal?"

Peter offered her a little gold gondola, of such exquisite workmanship that Patty gave a cry of delight.

"It's lovely!" she said. "Far too pretty for my 'memory chain.' I shall hang it on my watchguard."

She fastened it to the slender chain that held her watch, and smiled her thanks at Peter.

"I shall always think of you when I see it," she said; "and sometimes when I don't."

"I shall often think of you," he responded, "and shall look forward to meeting you again sometime, somewhere."

"Oh, come to New York," cried Patty; "you are coming, aren't you? And we'll have an Italian Days Reunion. Will you come, Floyd? And Flo?"

Pigeons and Poetry

The other gondola had drifted near again, and all were gaily promising to meet again in New York, when the quay of the railway station was reached, and everybody scrambled out.

Then, in the general flurry of looking after luggage, and getting seats in the train, there was no opportunity for further talk, but Peter said, earnestly:

"May I write to you, Patty? And will you answer my letters?"

"Oh, indeed I will! I'd love to hear from you, and of course I'll write back."

She gave him her card, and then after general farewells, intermingled with much nonsense and laughter, the Fairfield family, with Flo and Snippy, started for Rome.

CHAPTER XX

HOMEWARD BOUND

"I AM glad to be in Rome again," said Flo, as they once more sat at tea in the winter-garden of the hotel.

"Rome again, Rome again,
From a foreign shore,"

sang Patty; "but it doesn't seem like Rome with none of the other Wonderers here."

"And soon you're going, too;—oh, Patty, how I shall miss you!"

"I'll miss you, too, Flo dear. We've had good times together, haven't we?"

"Yes, indeed; I'll tell Lady Kitty all about it when I go back. I wish she could have been here with us."

"Yes, I hoped to have her; but I find she's a most uncertain personage. 'But what's the use of repining? to-morrow the sun may be shining!'"

"That's just you, all over, Patty! I believe

[292]

Homeward Bound

whoever composed that classic couplet must have known you. Do you never repine?"

"To tell you the awful truth, Flo, I don't quite know what that word means! Re-pine, I daresay, is to pine again. But you see I don't know how to pine the first time."

"Oh, Patty, you're a silly. But I can tell you, Mr. Peter Homer is going to do some pining after you."

"Really! Oh, Flo, how you embarrass me! I don't know where to hide my blushing face."

Saucy Patty was not embarrassed a bit, and Flo well knew it. But Flo had felt ever so tiny a tinge of jealousy at the evident interest Mr. Homer took in Patty, and she couldn't resist speaking of it.

"Don't you care, Patty, if he 'pines' for you?"

"I can't conscientiously say that I do," remarked Patty, with a judicial air. "He's free to pine if he enjoys it, I'm sure."

"Don't you care for him, specially, Patty?" went on Flo, determined to learn Patty's sentiment toward him.

"'Deed I don't! I like him a lot; he's one of the kindest and cleverest men I know. But as to 'liking him specially,' as you call it, I truly don't."

[293]

"Do you like any one specially?" persisted Flo.

"For goodness' gracious' sake, Flo! What is the matter with you? If you mean am I in love with anybody, I certainly am not, and don't expect to be for several hundred years yet! So there, now!"

"You're a funny girl, Patty. I expect to be married before I'm twenty."

"Well, I don't! And I don't want to. I may get married sometime in the distant future, if I find anybody I can 'pine' for. But I'm only eighteen now, and I can't be bothering with such matters."

"You'll be nineteen next spring."

"So I will! Well, come 'round then, and I'll talk to you about it. Have some tea?"

Flo and Patty had grown to be devoted friends, and both were really sorry that their parting was so near. A week's stay in Rome, and then the Fairfields would leave for Naples, and so home, by way of the Mediterranean, while Flo and Snippy would return at once to England.

The few days in Rome were devoted to farewell glimpses of favourite spots.

Patty, with Flo and Snippy, roamed round the Forum, and gazed at the Coliseum, and revisited many of the churches.

Homeward Bound

One evening Mr. Leland took them all to dinner in a delightful restaurant that overlooked the Palatine.

" I don't feel that I know my Palatine at all," said Patty, regretfully.

" Don't try to," said Mr. Leland, kindly. " Nobody really knows the Palatine, except the great scholars. When in the Palatine, just flounder about, and get the whole as a general picture of ruined glory. That's all you can do."

" Yes," agreed Patty. " I have a mixed-up memory of Livia's house, and Augustus's house, and the rest, and it doesn't really matter much who's who in the Palatine, does it? "

" Not a bit," said Mr. Leland; " but you can get a fair idea of the whole from this balcony."

He took Patty out on a balcony of the restaurant, used in summer as an open-air eating-place, and showed her the general view of the Palatine Hill. The others followed and listened with interest, while Mr. Leland pointed out the various ruins.

" It's splendid," said Nan, who was really more of a student of these things than Patty. " I shall always remember this view. It makes me feel nearer to ancient Rome than any other."

" I don't want you to get too near to ancient

[295]

Rome," said Mr. Fairfield, laughing, as he led her back indoors. " I want to keep you in the twentieth century for some time yet."

The last day in Rome, Patty was quite pensive,—for her. She went and sat on the Spanish Steps, she bought another large photograph of the Coliseum, and some more models of the Forum, which last, however, were broken to bits long before she reached home.

"I don't see why they don't make the silly things stronger," she said as, on reaching the hotel, she found two of the models in fragments.

" Because they're ruins," said Nan, consolingly. "Those old columns are nearly all in ruins, so it's fitting the little models should follow in their ways."

"Pshaw!" said Patty, flinging away the bits she had been trying to piece together. " There's no use getting any more of those; they smash if you look at them."

" Don't look at them then," said Nan, sweetly.

" I'll try to get some cast-iron ones,—that's the only kind of cast that won't break," said Patty, as she contented herself with photographs instead.

It was a lovely, sunshiny, autumn day when the Fairfields started for Naples.

Homeward Bound

"Our party grows smaller every time we move," said Patty to Flo. "Now we are dropping you and Snippy, but I suppose father and Nan and I will stick together till we reach New York."

"You'll have to," said practical Flo, "unless you leave one at Naples or Gibraltar."

"I wish you were going to Naples with us."

"I wish so too, Patty; but mother has written us to come home, and we really must go. But it has been a lovely pleasure trip with you, and I'm sure we'll meet again."

"Of course we shall. You surely must come to New York. Snippy can bring you, can't she?"

"Yes, indeed; Snippy could take me to the North Pole, if we decided to go."

"Well, see that she brings you to New York first. And now good-by, Flo, dearie. Write to me soon and often. Good-by, Snippy."

"Good-by, Miss Patty."

And then everybody said good-by to everybody else, and the travellers took the train, and Patty waved to Flo from the window, and called good-by again, and then they started, and the Fairfields were once more by themselves.

"You'll be dull, Patsy," said her father, "with only your own relatives to entertain you."

"What a libel, Daddy! Was I ever dull?"

"No, but there must be a first time for every-thing."

"Well, it won't be while I've you and my viva-cious stepmother for travelling companions."

And truly it didn't seem so. Nan and Patty fell to chattering, until Mr. Fairfield had diffi-culty in getting in a word edgewise. At last he took refuge in a newspaper, and finally fell asleep, while the loquacious two chattered on. They had not been much together while Patty had the younger girls about, and as they were really very good chums, they had much to talk over.

It seemed but a short trip, and before they knew it they were in Naples.

"I know I shall hate this place," said Patty, in tones of firm conviction. "It's the dirtiest and beggariest town in all Italy."

But as they started in an open cab for their hotel, Patty changed her mind.

"I don't see any dirt," she said. "They must have swept lately. And not a beggar has begged yet."

The driver pointed out the places of interest as they went along, and Patty's admiration steadily increased.

Homeward Bound

"I love Naples!" she said, finally. "Whoever jumped on it was all wrong."

"People don't jump on things in Italy," said her father, reprovingly.

"No, they're too lazy to jump," agreed Patty. "What hotel are we going to, Father?"

"To the Palace Hotel,—up on the Cliffs."

"They're all palace hotels in Italy, aren't they? Is that it, 'way up in the sky? How ever did it perch itself up on that high place?"

"Spread its wings and flew up there," said her father.

"I think it went up there to get a good view of the bay," said Nan.

"The Bay of Naples!" cried Patty, standing up in the cab to look behind her. "I've seen it on postcards, and it's almost as blue, really. Oh, people! Isn't it great!"

"Sit down, Patty, you'll break your neck."

"Not in this gently moving chaise. Oh, we're climbing this great hill. See how the road winds, and how the cliffs——"

"Beetle," said Nan.

"Yes, that's just it! These are beetling crags. I never realised what that meant before. And see this strange thing! It must be the ruins of an old dungeon. See how it juts and

[299]

slopes straight up the mountain. A castle, ruined by an earthquake, probably. What is it, driver?"

"A landslide, madame."

"Oh," said Patty, in disgust, "I thought it was a ruined building."

Arrived at the top of the really high hill, they alighted at the entrance to the hotel. And a peculiar entrance it was. First they walked through a long, straight marble-lined corridor that had been cut horizontally into the cliff. From this a vertical elevator-shaft was cut straight up to the hotel itself, many feet above. The ride up in the elevator seemed interminable, but at last they stepped out into a beautiful glass-enclosed parlour, from which Naples could be seen below them in every direction.

"Oh! oh!" exclaimed Patty, running from the view of the bay to that of Vesuvius, and then to the city view.

"I never saw such a fascinating place! Stay over another steamer, Daddy; don't let's go home yet."

"We'll settle that question later. Now, let's go and find our rooms, Puss, and then you can come back here. The views will probably keep an hour or so."

Homeward Bound

They followed an attendant through long corridors and labyrinthine ways, and came at last to their rooms, which looked out upon the beautiful bay, with Capri smiling sunnily across the blue, and Vesuvius standing calmly on the other side. Patty, in ecstasies of delight, could scarcely wait to unpack her things, and danced into Nan's room, exclaiming anew at the beauties of the hotel, the city, and Italy in general.

"You goose!" said Nan. "One would think you'd never seen anything at all before. Do you like it better than Venice, or Rome?"

"No,—not better," said Patty, slowly, "but you see I didn't expect to like it at all, and so it's such a surprise."

"Well, run and put on a fresh frock for tea, and then you can rhapsodise, while I refresh myself with tea-cakes."

"I'm hungry too," said Patty, "but then I always am." She flew away to dress, and soon the family sat in the glass-protected tea-room, enjoying strange little Neapolitan cakes, that all declared the best in the world.

After tea, Mr. Fairfield said they would have time for a short drive before dinner. Patty was delighted at this prospect, and skipped away

[301]

for her hat and cloak. The rickety old cab made her laugh, but as they drove along she saw none better, so decided that they were a style peculiar to Naples.

They visited no museums or palaces, as Mr. Fairfield said it was but a preliminary drive, and they must return for dinner.

So back they went soon, climbing the high hill slowly, though it seemed to Patty not nearly so high nor so steep as the first time they drove up. The long trip up in the elevator was unpleasant to Nan, who feared an accident; but Patty said, "Nonsense! it's just like the subway up on end; and no danger of meeting another train."

Dinner was rather a pretentious function in the hotel, so our party donned evening dress, and came down at eight o'clock, to find the gorgeous and brilliantly lighted dining-room well-filled. Lovely strains of music came from an orchestra behind a screen of palms, and the viands were of the best.

"It *is* a lovely place," said Nan; "I quite agree with you, Patty, and I'm surprised at it all, too."

After dinner they strolled about in the various attractive rooms, and Patty thought she'd never tire of the beautiful view of Naples by night, that was spread out below them. The street lights looked like long strings of jewels, and the brightly lighted houses added to the splendour of the scene. On the other side was the bay, misty now, and pierced here and there with the shipping lights.

Long after they had gone to their rooms Patty sat at her window, enthralled with the strange beauty, so different from all else she had seen that it seemed like an enchanted land.

After several days of sight-seeing in and around Naples, which had included trips to Vesuvius and to Amalfi, Mr. Fairfield called a council of war to decide upon further plans.

"I've passage engaged, as you know," he said, "for December first. This will get us home about the middle of the month, and give us a little time to get our breath before the Christmas holidays. But if you two girls prefer, we can change our tickets and stay here till the fifteenth."

"That wouldn't get us home by Christmas Day," said Patty, thoughtfully.

"No, we'd be on the Atlantic on Christmas. But we must take one steamer or the other."

"Well, I'll leave it to Nan," said Patty; "but

[303]

personally, I'd hate to spend Christmas on an ocean liner! It doesn't seem patriotic."

"I agree to all that," said Nan. "I love Naples, but I'd rather go next week, and so be home in time to look after a little Christmas celebration of some sort, than to stay here longer."

"All right, then," said Mr. Fairfield. "My inclinations are to go on the first. So we'll consider it settled, and put in all the fun we can these few days that are left."

So the three spent the rest of the time in seeing Naples thoroughly. They visited the Aquarium, and the Royal Palace, and the National Museum. They visited Capri, and they drove out to Posilipo, and Camaldoli; and every day they grew more fond of the beautiful environs that surrounded Naples. But their thoughts began to turn to home and Christmas, and reunion of friends, and delightful as their pleasure trip had been, it was with a satisfied feeling in their hearts that they at last went aboard the great steamer that was to land them in New York.

"Good-by, beautiful Italy," said Patty, waving her handkerchief as they steamed away. "I'll come back some time,—but I think not very soon. I'm a bit homesick for my ain countree."